A Celtic Knot

Ana Corman

ISBN: 1451593457
ISBN-13: 9781451593457

Acknowledgments

BREAST CANCER HAS TOUCHED SO MANY LIVES. It's an experience that has terrified, challenged, strengthened, galvanized, and united us. So many women have stood strong and proven we will not be defeated. I dedicate this book to all breast-cancer survivors and their loved ones who walked that difficult road together. Triumphantly.

My mother is a breast-cancer survivor, and her experience sparked the creation of this book. Mom, I love you and celebrate your life.

This story was created with the undying support and encouragement of my partner, Catherine. Your unconditional love feeds my imagination and fuels my desire to write. I cherish the intricately woven life I share with you. You fulfill me and make me complete. The Celtic knot symbolizes eternity—the eternity I plan to share with you. I love you with all my heart.

A Celtic Knot would not be what it is without the guidance, creative input, and patient teaching of my editor, Lydia Bird. You challenged me and opened my mind to so many possibilities, allowing the story to take its final shape. You've made me a better writer. I thank you for that gift.

Also by Ana Corman

Tender Heart
Bradley Bay
Love Light

One

CATHERINE CAREFULLY BROUGHT THE HOT MUG of latte to her lips before gently blowing away the steam. She held the mug in both hands and leaned her hip against the customer-service counter. She looked up to the second level of the bookstore and saw several dozen customers browsing the well-stocked aisles. Her eyes followed the child gripping tightly to her mother's hand with her Dora doll safely tucked under her other arm. They slowly descended the wide staircase and headed for the checkout counter, then joined the four other people in line as the little girl looked back at Catherine and smiled. Catherine winked at her.

A heavy book hit the floor with a dull thud and Catherine looked across the bookstore to the coffee shop. Two college-age students scrambled to collect their scattered papers and textbook. The lunch-hour crowds were slowly clearing out of the coffee shop, but half the tables were still full of patrons. Crystal and Summer worked fluidly and swiftly behind the counter serving the customers with their usual bubbly charm.

This year would be their tenth anniversary, and Catherine couldn't believe they'd been open that long. Cocoa Cream was her vision. She'd always dreamed of a combination coffee shop and new-and-used bookstore. Its success spoke clearly in the steady stream of regulars who came in for a cup of specialty coffee or tea and to browse the rows of bookshelves.

Catherine took a sip of her latte before setting her mug down on the counter. She frowned as the St. Patrick's Day banner across the front of the customer-service desk bounced once then twice. She moved her coffee mug aside and looked over the edge. A clawless paw gripped the edge of the decoration as a pair of deep sea green eyes looked up at her. "Maya, cut that out. You're going to ruin the decoration. Now get up here right now."

Cocoa Cream's resident snow white Persian leapt gracefully onto the countertop and rubbed herself against Catherine's belly. "You're such a little imp. Now behave yourself, before I introduce you to the coffee grinder." Maya dropped down onto her belly with her front paws curled under her chest like a royal kitty as Catherine massaged her face and neck. She heard a loud crash of several books and a long hushed curse from the mystery section. "Are you all right, Laura?"

A tall, slender woman poked her auburn head around the antique timepiece that proudly stood guard between the horror and mystery books. "I'm fine. I didn't need that toe anyway."

"Do you need a hand?"

"No. I'll be done in a minute. Don't you have to get going to that doctor's appointment?"

Catherine glanced at the grandfather clock. "Pretty soon. Mom's appointment's at two. She's in the back room organizing the new shipment of romance books. She'll come get me when she's ready. It's probably a good way for her to burn off some nervous energy."

Laura grabbed an armful of books and made her way to the customer-service desk. Catherine took the books from her and eased them onto the countertop. "We do have carts you can use to haul these books around, you know. You're liable to give yourself a hernia, and then that lawyer husband of yours will sue me for every last penny I have."

Laura's laughter filled the air. "If my pregnancies didn't give me a hernia, nothing will. Besides, Kevin loves you as much as he loves me. Your piggy bank is safe from him."

"There you both are."

Catherine turned as her mother approach. Dana O'Grady had just turned fifty-five and looked at least ten years younger. Her dark flowing hair and creamy Irish complexion were flawless. She exuded boundless energy and a fighting Irish spirit that awed and inspired Catherine.

Catherine noticed the frown creasing her mother's forehead. "What's wrong, Mom?"

Dana gently rubbed Maya's chin. "I just got off the phone with Ruth. Her mother fell and broke her hip this morning. She's flying out to Phoenix to be with her. We'll be seen by her partner Dr. Carrington this afternoon."

"How awful. I hope she'll be all right."

"Me, too. I'm worried about both of them. I told her to call and let us know what's happening."

Catherine laid her hand on her mother's shoulder. "These appointments are stressful enough for you when we see Dr. Ratcliff. Why don't we change your appointment till she gets back? We don't know this Dr. Carrington, and he doesn't know your history."

"The he is a she, Dr. Olivia Carrington, and I do know her. I've met with several of her patients in the Comfort Program. I really like her."

Catherine was proud of the work her mother did with other cancer patients, but it wasn't something they talked about often.

"Anyway, there's no way I'm prolonging this appointment for another day. All Dr. Carrington has to do is tell us the results of my mammogram. Hopefully it'll all be good and we can run out of that office and not return for another year."

Catherine saw that determined look in her mother's light blue eyes and knew the subject was settled. "All right. I'll grab my purse if you're ready to go."

Dana inhaled deeply. "I hate this feeling."

Catherine reached for her mother's hand and held it gently. "I know you do, Mom."

Dana squeezed her hand and forced a smiled. "Let's go get this over with."

Laura stepped around the counter and hugged Dana close. "Good luck. I'm praying for you. I'll call you later to hear the good results."

Dana kissed her cheek. "I appreciate your prayers, Laura. Thank you."

Catherine took Maya's furry little face in her hands and touched her nose to the beautiful squished face. "Be a good guard kitty and keep the store safe from mean people and dangerous lesbians."

Two

THE CLICK CLICKING OF THE PEN shattered the quiet of the examination room. Dana peered over her *Better Homes and Gardens* at her daughter sitting in a chair a few feet away. Catherine's legs were crossed and her right leg was swinging to the clicking rhythm of the pen. She was holding a pamphlet on breast-cancer research and Dana knew she was not absorbing a word. This cold room had the same nerve-shattering affect on both of them as it had five years ago.

The clicking continued as Dana placed the magazine down on the examination table beside her. She wrapped the flimsy, scratchy hospital gown tighter around her. "Catherine, please stop."

Catherine glanced up surprised, then looked at the pen and tucked it in the inside pocket of her jacket. "Sorry, Mom."

"I don't know which one of us is more nervous, me or you."

Catherine tossed the brochure on the counter and stood up. "I hate this place. I just hate that you have to come back here year after year for your checkups only to be reminded of what you went through."

Dana slipped her hand into her daughter's. "I love you."

"I love you too, Mom."

Both women turned as they heard hushed voices outside the door. A sharp, loud knock sounded before the door opened and two men and two women in lab coats with stethoscopes draped around their necks entered the room. A middle-aged man with slicked-back hair, a long greasy ponytail, and a receding hairline stood before Dana.

"Mrs. O'Grady, I'm Dr. Snyder. I'm the new resident in the surgical oncology service. As you heard, Dr. Ratcliff felt she needed to tend to a family situation. Behind me are three medical students who will be observing my techniques. We're on a very tight schedule today, so I'd like to begin."

Dana hugged the gown tight across her chest. She looked over his shoulder at the scrubbed young faces of the bewildered medical students. Catherine stood ramrod stiff at her side.

Dr. Snyder sighed heavily as he thumbed through her file. He licked his thumb and flipped through several more pages without even looking up at her. He slapped the file closed and tucked it under his arm. He turned his back on Dana and Catherine and faced the medical students.

"Mrs. O'Grady is a fifty-five-year-old patient of Dr. Ratcliff's. She was diagnosed five years ago with infiltrating ductal carcinoma of the right breast. This type of breast cancer is found in seventy percent of the women diagnosed with breast cancer. The cancer cells originate in the ducts and start invading the surrounding fatty tissue. The prognosis depends on how fast the cancer is growing, if it has spread to any organs and which ones, and the response to treatment. Mrs. O'Grady had a lumpectomy and radiation therapy and is currently on Tamoxifen. If there are no questions, I would like to proceed to the examination of the breast."

Dr. Snyder dropped the file onto the counter beside Dana and looked at her with beady eyes. "Mrs. O'Grady, will you take off your gown?"

Dana wrapped the gown tighter across her chest. "I'll do no such thing. Where's Dr. Carrington? She's the one we expected to see today."

Catherine stepped in front of her mother, forcing Dr. Snyder to take a stumbling step backward. "Who the hell do you think you are? In five years we've never been seen by anyone but Dr. Ratcliff, and we're not about to tolerate this kind of treatment. As for your precious tight schedule, we've been patiently sitting in this freezing-cold room for forty-five minutes—if you think your time is any more valuable than ours, you're sadly mistaken."

Dana wasn't sure if she should stop her daughter or applaud. And Catherine wasn't finished with Dr. Snyder. "My mother is not just another breast. She's a breast-cancer survivor who's endured countless physical examinations that have left her feeling completely stripped of her modesty. I will not stand here and let you treat her like just another patient who you need to rush along on an assembly line. So, no, she will not take her gown off. I suggest you take your king-size ego and pathetic manners and go find yourself a breast implant and see if it wants to play your macho games."

Hurrying down the hall, Olivia Carrington could hear the barrage of furious words from inside the examination room. Could this day possibly get any worse? She was worried about Ruth and her mother, and hadn't had a chance to call and check on them. She'd worked right through the lunch hour and was in dire need of a bathroom break. She felt pulled in a million directions. The argument spilling from the examination room was clearly one more fire she would need to put out.

She opened the door and entered the crowded room. To her right, Dr. Snyder stood cowering with his medical students. Dana O'Grady sat nervously on the edge of the examination table. Next to her stood the young woman clearly responsible for the angry words. Dana O'Grady's daughter was stunning, despite the talons ready to strike—slim, with short auburn hair and eloquent eyes. Her protective stance exuded her profound closeness to her mother. Olivia forced herself to look away from this high-spirited beauty and moved next to Dana. She gently took her hands. "Hello, Dana. It's a pleasure to see you, as always."

"I'm so glad to see you, Olivia. However, we're not so happy with your choice of residents."

"So I heard."

Dana smiled and gestured to Catherine. "Dr. Olivia Carrington, I'd like you to meet my daughter, Catherine."

Their eyes locked. A myriad of intense emotions swirled in Catherine's sea blue eyes. Olivia cautiously extended her hand. "Hello, Catherine."

Catherine folded her arms across her chest. "How nice of you to take the time to join us, Dr. Carrington. Who the hell gave you permission to let that idiot resident see us? We realize you must be busy, but your decision to send in this buffoon shows very poor judgment. If you don't have time for my mother, then we'll just get our things and come back when Dr. Ratcliff returns to her practice."

Olivia slowly pulled her hand back and tucked it into the pocket of her gray slacks. "That won't be necessary." She looked over at Dr. Snyder and the medical students standing against the far wall. "I never gave anyone permission to enter this room without me. I told you to review Mrs. O'Grady's file and wait for me outside so I could ask her if you could join me in her appointment."

Dr. Snyder grabbed his belt and hiked it higher against the underside of his heaving belly. "I thought I'd come in and get started so we could speed things along. We're already behind in our schedule."

Olivia took a slow measured step closer to Dr. Snyder. "Don't think, Dr. Snyder. Do exactly as I say. You have obviously offended the O'Grady family, and that upsets me terribly. You disobeyed what I said. You came in here of your own accord without Mrs. O'Grady's permission, and that is a direct violation of her patient privacy. Now, I want you all out of this examination room and I want you to wait for me in my office. Don't touch another file, don't go near another patient. Have I made myself perfectly clear?"

Dr. Snyder had a look of pure shock on his face. "Yes, perfectly clear." He slowly backed out of the room and was followed by the three medical students.

The door closed quietly behind them as Olivia turned to Dana and Catherine. "I don't know how to begin to apologize for Dr. Snyder's behavior. No woman who comes to our practice should ever be treated like that, and I'm so sorry it had to be you."

She ventured a glance toward Catherine and was met with a withering look.

"I'm not impressed by anything I've seen in this office so far, Dr. Carrington," Catherine said. "See what you can do to change that."

Olivia raised her eyebrows and turned back to Dana. "I think we better get started with your appointment. Otherwise your fiery daughter is liable to disintegrate me with that look in her eyes."

Dana laughed. She knew very little about Olivia Carrington, but had liked her the moment they had met. She was fiercely dedicated to her work, leaving Dana wondering how much energy she had for a personal life. She cared deeply about her patients and their success. Ruth had been thrilled to bring the talented young oncologist into her practice.

Olivia gestured to the file on the counter. "Let's get to the wonderful news of the day. Your mammogram looks perfect."

Dana felt the relief wash through her. "Oh, Olivia. That's just the news I wanted to hear. That means we can go home now." Dana started to ease off the examination table.

Olivia laughed and placed her hands on Dana's knees. "Nice try, but not so fast. I need to do your breast exam before you go anywhere. I wouldn't want Catherine calling me an incompetent buffoon."

Catherine narrowed her eyes. "Since we're on the subject of competence, how long have you been working with Dr. Ratcliff, anyway?"

"I've been a board-certified surgical oncologist for four years. I went to med school here in San Diego. Dr. Ratcliff recruited me from my residency in New York, and I feel blessed to be a part of this oncology team. I'm particularly glad to see how well your mother has done with her recovery. I know how much you've been through."

"Without Catherine, I often wonder how I would've survived," Dana said. "She was there with me every step of the way. We've grown closer because of my cancer."

"I'm so glad you had each other. And I'm so appreciative of the work you've done the past couple of years with women in the Comfort Program. You've been a huge help and inspiration to them."

Dana reached for Catherine's hand. She knew this subject was a difficult one for her daughter. "I had Catherine. Not everyone has that kind of love and support during such a difficult time. At first I felt I wasn't ready or emotionally strong enough to be of help to anyone, but now I really enjoy helping other women through this difficult journey."

Olivia noticed how Catherine looked at her mother and then quickly looked away. She wanted to know what made her so uncomfortable. She felt intrigued by her quick temper and complex emotions. She craved to understand the many layers of Catherine O'Grady. This was not the time or the place. Olivia forced her mind back to the task at hand.

She squeezed Dana's shoulder. "Are you ready for your breast exam?"

"I am."

Olivia helped Dana to lie back comfortably with her arms over her head. She rubbed her hands together several times to warm them. "Have you been doing your monthly self-exams?"

"Religiously."

"Good girl." Olivia began her examination, feeling for lumps in Dana's breasts, underarms, and collarbone area. "You've been on your Tamoxifen for five years now, haven't you?"

"Yes. It's hard to believe."

"I'm thrilled that you've made it to this milestone without recurrence. This means you can stop taking your Tamoxifen."

Dana linked her fingers behind her head. "Do you mind if I also talk to Ruth before I stop taking it?"

"Not at all. I would recommend it." Olivia moved her hands to Dana's axilla. "Catherine, have you had a mammogram since your mother's diagnosis?"

"I've had two done and they were both normal. Dr. Ratcliff said I should have one annually."

Olivia moved to the other breast. "She's right. I'm glad you're following her advice."

"I trust her. She even had me bring in my mammogram films to my mother's appointments so she could see them herself. She's been terrific to both of us."

Olivia gently palpated Dana's abdomen. "You wouldn't feel that way if she'd pawned two mischievous little beasts off on you while she's gone."

Dana laughed. "Oh, the ferrets! Olivia, you're in for a very entertaining time with them."

"We'll see. She dropped them off at my house on her way to the airport. Her beloved furry rodents better behave themselves, or I'll pack them in a UPS box and ship them off to Phoenix."

"I highly recommend you not do that. That could well be the end of your very promising career."

Olivia laughed as she took her stethoscope from around her neck. "You're probably right. I really do love working here so I think I'm stuck with Abbott and Costello till Ruth gets back."

She placed her stethoscope in her ears and listened to Dana's lungs and heart, then hooked the instrument back around her neck. "Catherine, do you have any more questions for me?"

"No. This is not meant as any offense to you, but I'm glad we had someone with Dr. Ratcliff's years of experience care for my mother."

Olivia looked down at Dana. "That's all I needed today— to meet your blunt, ego-bashing daughter. There's no catching a break with her. She's one tough nut to crack."

Dana grinned broadly. "You're going to need to bring out the big guns on my little coconut."

Olivia gathered Dana's gown to cover her breasts and helped her to sit up. "Catherine, you have every right to feel that way. Dr. Ratcliff has been an exceptional surgical oncologist for twenty years. Her experience is vast, and I hope to learn everything I can from her."

She turned back to Dana. "Your mammogram is negative and your breast exam is negative of any masses. I now give you my permission to escape from this office. It's really a pleasure to see you and tell you that everything looks great." She fought back the desire to stay in the room, to stay in the presence of Catherine O'Grady, rather than plunging back into the fray of a chaotic day. She walked to the door and took hold of the knob. "Dana, did you get the email about the lecture series this afternoon?"

Dana faltered. "I did. I was pleased to see that you'd be speaking. I haven't missed a lecture yet, but I think Catherine would probably prefer to head back to the bookstore."

Catherine hesitated. "You shouldn't miss it because of me." She swallowed hard and turned to Olivia. "What's the subject of your lecture?"

Olivia was perplexed by her discomfort. "I'll be speaking about complimentary therapies for breast cancer. The feedback for the lecture series has been very positive. Ruth feels we need to educate medical professionals as well as the general public if we're going to beat this beast. Our patients benefit from the information and that's what means a lot to us." Olivia eased the door open. "I'll see you on your way out, Dana." She was partially through the door when she turned back. "Oh, Catherine, I'll rummage through our drawers and see if I can find a breast implant so the big jerk can practice his machismo."

Dana failed to suppress her laughter at the scorching look her daughter gave Olivia.

Catherine narrowed her eyes as the door closed. "I hope her lecture this afternoon is much more impressive than her sense of humor."

Three

CATHERINE AND DANA ENTERED the noisy amphitheater and carefully made their way up the steps to two empty seats. "I can't believe the size of this crowd," Catherine said. "There must be at least a hundred and fifty people here."

"Maybe they know that Dr. Carrington's lecture is better than her sense of humor."

Catherine glared at her mother. "Smart ass."

Dana settled into the plush seat. "Thank you for coming with me, sweetheart. I know it's uncomfortable for you to spend so much time around topics related to cancer."

Catherine looked away. "I wish it wasn't, Mom. I wish I could be more supportive to your causes."

It had surprised Dana when Catherine agreed to attend the lecture. Catherine did her best to bury their experience with cancer and move forward. Dana respected that, but she felt differently. She'd beat her cancer and wanted to help other women find the same success, to help make this experience as tolerable as possible. It wasn't always easy, but if that was the purpose of her breast cancer, then she'd continue to help in any way she could.

She touched her daughter's hand. "You're the most wonderful daughter a mother could ask for. I love you for who you are and all the wonderful support you give me each and every day. Look at how you protected me from that big buffoon back there."

"I wasn't about to let him or anyone else treat you that way."

Catherine looked around the amphitheater, wondering why she'd agreed to attend this lecture. How many of these women had recently been diagnosed with breast cancer? How many of them loved someone who had the disease? She could imagine what they were going through all too well, and she hated that feeling.

Olivia stepped onto the stage below them. Catherine felt a flush of excitement. That irritated her. If she was honest with herself, the reason she'd agreed to be here was because Olivia intrigued her. She watched Olivia connect her laptop to the projector, moving effortlessly around her equipment. She was slim and graceful, with thick dark curls that bounced to her mid back. Catherine was drawn to her beauty, and that made her even more exasperated by Dr. Olivia Carrington. How could a woman she just met send so many emotions raging within her? She wasn't sure she wanted to know.

Olivia slipped a wireless microphone around her ear and positioned the slim wire before her mouth. She thanked the technician helping her and moved to the center of the stage.

"Ladies and gentlemen, I think we're ready to begin."

The hum of voices stopped and everyone settled into a seat.

"I'm Dr. Olivia Carrington, and I'd like to thank you all for attending my lecture today on complementary therapies. I'm flattered to see such a large crowd but I hope you all weren't expecting to get a free massage today."

Everyone laughed.

"A complementary therapy is any therapy that complements the mainstream medical care for breast cancer. I believe that the human mind is a powerful healer and any therapy a woman chooses that will help to infuse her body with that healing power is a wonderful thing. We as women need to feel in control of our own bodies and our ability to overcome any illness. From acupuncture to massage therapy, aromatherapy to prayer, complementary therapies can strengthen our immune systems, treat symptoms, and improve our quality of life. Many women have stated that these therapies make them feel better and stronger."

Catherine settled back into her seat and listened intently as Olivia articulately went on to describe each different therapy and its benefits, moving about the stage and using computer images to keep the crowd's rapt attention.

"Women diagnosed with breast cancer endure so much during their treatment regime of surgery, radiation, and or chemotherapy," she concluded. "If any of these complementary therapies help to comfort you physically, emotionally, and mentally then I'm all for it. It's your own personal decision as to what may work for you. I feel it's important that women know that these therapies are available to them. I'd like to now turn the microphones over to you and try to answer any questions you may have."

The lights came on in the amphitheater, Olivia easily answered several questions and had the crowd laughing at her responses.

Catherine raised her hand and saw a man in the aisle pass her a microphone. He signaled for her to stand when it was her turn. As her eyes met Olivia's, she felt an uncomfortable tightening in her belly.

"You have a question for me, Catherine O'Grady?"

"I do. I thought your lecture was excellent, but you focused on complementary therapies and never mentioned alternative therapies. I'm just wondering why."

"That's an excellent question, Catherine. I didn't mention alternative therapies because there's a huge difference between alternative therapy and complementary therapy, when often those terms are used interchangeably. Alternative therapies are used instead of our conventional Western medical treatment. Examples of that are drugs that are illegal in the United States and commonly experimented with in other countries. Nothing has been proven with their use. They have not been studied scientifically and the risks and complications are unknown. Another example of alternative medicine is choosing to use a special diet rather than the surgery, radiation, or chemotherapy that we would prescribe in our practice.

"The huge problem is that women are led to believe in these alternative therapies and they have not proven to cure cancer or cause remission. They only delay the medical treatment that you need to receive."

"So, because alternative therapies go completely against your conventional Western-medicine upbringing you decide not to discuss them in your lecture?"

A low hum enveloped the room as Olivia took several steps across the stage.

"I won't apologize for my education and subsequently my beliefs in the strength and success of our mainstream medical care. I've operated on hundreds of women and seen them succeed with radiation and chemotherapy. No other therapy can offer that kind of success, and successful therapy is what we strive for."

"I'm not asking for your apologies, Dr. Carrington. We as women are only asking for all the information available to us. We'll make our own informed consent. You have to have more faith in us to know that for the most part we'll weed through what's right and wrong and make the decisions that are right for us."

The silence was deafening as Catherine handed back the microphone. The applause in the room started slowly and built to a steady beat. Catherine took her seat as her mother took her hand and squeezed it tight. From the stage, Olivia gave her a piercing look that unsettled her. Olivia was clearly angry, but there was something else in the look that Catherine couldn't interpret.

"Point taken. Some types of complementary or alternative therapies may interfere or be harmful when used with a treatment regime already prescribed by your conventional Western medicine doctor. I just ask that before you decide to use any of these therapies, please speak to your doctor so you can discuss the possible risks and benefits. Also check with your insurance company to see which of these therapies are covered. Are there any other questions?"

Olivia answered questions for another twenty minutes before she ended the lecture. Everyone gave her a standing ovation before they began to file slowly out of the amphitheater.

Catherine sat stiffly in her chair.

"Are you okay?" Dana asked.

"I'm okay. I believe that Olivia has now officially taken me off her Christmas card list."

Dana laughed. "Why don't you go talk to her?"

Catherine stared at her mother. "Are you kidding? I don't think Dr. Olivia Carrington wants to hear another word from me."

Dana smiled. "I know you, darling. You're going to beat yourself up till you make peace between you and Olivia. If you do want to talk to her, I wouldn't mind going up to the fifth floor to visit with one of Ruth's patients. She had a lump removed yesterday. I wouldn't be long. I'd just like to make sure she has everything she needs."

Catherine closed her eyes. She could at least give her mother the time she needed to support another woman going through surgery. It had been a long time since Dana talked about the women she visited. Catherine could show her how proud she was of her.

"You should do that, Mom. You can call me on your cell phone when you're done. We can meet in the front foyer of the hospital."

Dana leaned in close and kissed her daughter's cheek. "Thank you, sweetheart. I'll see you in a little while."

Catherine watched her mother make her way along the aisle and climb down the steps. A group of women walked off the stage after talking to Olivia. The two who remained— one of them pregnant—stood intimately close to her as they talked together, then hugged her before leaving the stage. Catherine recognized them as customers she'd seen in Cocoa Cream and was intrigued by their closeness with Olivia. She rose from her seat. "It's now or never," she told herself.

Catherine made her way toward the stage as Olivia gathered her equipment. She found the stairs along the wing and slowly climbed them.

She stood close by and watched Olivia wind the electrical cord and place it on the bottom of her cart. The amphitheater felt cold and hollow. "We're the only ones left behind, Dr. Carrington. Please feel free to tell me why my question infuriated you so much."

Olivia stayed with her back to Catherine and removed her jacket. She carefully draped it across the metal cart and slowly turned to face her. "Alternative therapy is a very touchy subject with me, Catherine, as you may have noticed. I don't believe in it and I don't want women to waste their time looking into it. I want them to spend what energy they have on positive therapies that complement their medical treatment. Not hinder the best care they can get."

"I agree with you, but I also feel we have a right to investigate all the treatments available. When my mother was first diagnosed, we read every piece of literature we could get our hands on. With Dr. Ratcliff's help, we made the best decisions we could for her treatment. We felt comfortable with our plan because we'd exhausted all the information at our disposal. We felt in control of her healing process. You can't hold back information from women because of your own personal beliefs, Dr. Carrington. That will only leave them resentful and distrusting of your motives."

Olivia took a step toward Catherine. "I offer my patients a book of information on all the complementary therapies I presented today. I give them safe, proven information and let them integrate anything that works for them. I support their choices when I know it'll help their treatment regime." Olivia shoved her hands into her pockets. "Why do I have the feeling this has so much more to do with your mother's appointment this afternoon than my presentation? I know you were angry with me, Catherine, but I'm surprised you tried to embarrass me in front of my audience."

"My question had nothing to do with embarrassing you in front of your audience, Dr. Carrington, or about my mother's appointment. I would've thought you had stronger self-esteem than that. My question had nothing to do with you at all. It's purely about access to information. My mother feels comfortable spending time with women who are newly diagnosed. I don't. I have a difficult time with their fear and anguish. But I own a bookstore, and I make sure the shelves are stocked with all the current literature about breast cancer. I may sound cowardly to you compared to my mother, but that's where I feel I can help. It's my comfort zone."

"That's hardly cowardly, Catherine. That's very admirable and a huge contribution to what women need when they're diagnosed." She moved closer. "But why would you even consider alternative therapies?"

Catherine took a deep breath. She felt hesitant to talk about this with Olivia, and yet somehow she needed to. "I looked into alternative therapy because I'm scared. My family history has me terrified. My father died three months after he was diagnosed with stomach cancer."

"I read that in your mothers chart. I'm so sorry."

Catherine looked away from that expression of pure compassion. "Your traditional Western medicine has worked wonderfully for my mother but nothing worked for my father. Western medicine only intensified his pain and made his last months with us excruciating. We did that to him. I have every right to want to know about alternative therapies." Catherine fought back her tears. "When my father died, I was so angry and grief stricken that I lost faith in your wonderful Western medicine. Why can't we find a cure for cancer, Olivia? We pour money into prevention, early detection, treatment, and research and yet people are still dying."

"I'm not the enemy, Catherine."

"I know that, Olivia. But in our stressed-out, agonized minds you're the only enemy we can see. We can't see the cancer but we can see the people who put us through so much grief and pain."

"I'm on your side, Catherine. I pour my energy into fighting this disease with proven methods. I have to have faith in the people who are devoting their lives to finding the answers to questions that haven't been answered yet. The world is engaged in this fight against cancer. You have to believe in what has been proven by the numbers of successful cases. Your mother is a perfect example of that. I'm just sorry there couldn't have been more to offer your father."

"I'm sorry, too. He was an amazing man and an incredible father. His life was wonderful and his death was horrible. What if I'm next, Olivia? Will Western medicine fail me, too?" Before Olivia could answer, Catherine's cell phone rang. She wiped at her eyes and looked at the display. "My mother's waiting for me. I have to go."

As she turned for the stairs, Olivia reached for her arm. "I'm sorry you're upset, Catherine. I'm just beginning to understand why. If there's anything I can do for you, any way I can help ease your fear, I wish you'd let me know."

"These are my issues to deal with. Unfortunately, they just keep rearing their ugly heads. Good-bye, Olivia. Thank you for being so kind to my mother today."

Four

DANA CAREFULLY REACHED through the bed of pruned rosebushes and pulled out her *San Diego Union-Tribune*. She slapped it hard against her thigh several times, then stepped back to admire the row of rosebushes running along the deep front porch. They were her pride and joy. She loved gardening and watching things grow. She could plant things with total abandon and the disorder always bred beauty. Bright green shoots had already pushed their way up in the flowerbeds bordering the walkway leading to the house, a sure sign that spring was on its way. Soon they'd be laden with yellow freesias and daylilies, divided by groups of white daffodils and grape hyacinths. The massive jacaranda tree in the front yard would not bloom its gorgeous lavender flowers till June. Dana couldn't wait for that yearly event.

She remembered the day the previous owners had contacted her to sell this wonderful house. As she'd strolled up the walkway, she knew she had come home. It was a spiritual connection. The location was perfect, just north of Balboa Park. She and Aidan moved in and Catherine was born a year later. Dana loved its old-world charm and mystique. It was a solid brick bungalow built in 1925, with stone pillars and sloped roofs. It had been a financial stretch at the time, as she began her real estate career and Aidan was struggling to get his accounting firm off the ground. But it was worth all the penny-pinching in those early years. They'd chosen to make renovations instead of moving into something bigger when finances were on more solid ground. Dana was so grateful they stayed.

It was getting dusky and Dana felt a slight chill with the cool breeze. It had been overcast and dreary all week but today had been a beautiful bright day in the high sixties. A glorious day for late February in San Diego. Dana tucked the newspaper under her arm, unlocked the front door, and set her mail and paper on the hall table among the stacks of magazines. She needed to tidy up that mess. She could hear Aidan chastising her for her collection of magazines that she could never get rid of. It extended to her stack of cookbooks in the kitchen and scrap-booking supplies in the spare bedroom. Catherine threatened to call the fire department and report her mother as a fire hazard. She shook her head and laughed. One of these days she would make Catherine proud. Thank God her daughter was a neat freak and meticulously organized like her father.

Dana was so grateful to be home. Catherine had dropped her off at the bookstore after they shared a wonderful meal at their favorite Thai restaurant. She'd hoped that Catherine would feel better after talking to Olivia, but it looked like it only made matters worse. She listened to her throughout dinner try to make sense of their interaction. Dana had never seen her daughter so befuddled by a woman before. She hoped she'd feel better after a good night's sleep. Knowing her daughter, the possibilities were slim. She'd call to check on her before turning in for the night.

She checked that she had no phone messages and set the teakettle to boil. She reached into the antique hutch and pulled out her favorite bone china teacup. She loved the antiques that she and Aidan had collected to fill their home. The memories flooded back where they purchased each piece and how they haggled over prices with the dealers.

The house phone rang. She smiled at the name on the display.

"Hello, Dr. Ruth Ratcliff. How's your mother?" She removed the teakettle from the stove.

"She's doing well, considering. She has a brand new hip and she's resting comfortably."

Dana walked into the great room and settled into a chocolate suede loveseat. "I'm so glad. I've been thinking about both of you all day. I stopped into the church today and lit a candle for her. I also lit a candle to pray that you'll never abandon me for one of my appointments with you again."

"That's one of the reasons I called. I'm so sorry about what happened with Dr. Snyder, Dana."

"No harm was done. Olivia handled the situation beautifully. It's good she came in when she did or Catherine might have ripped out his tongue and shoved it back down his throat."

"Well, in that case I wish Olivia had been delayed a little longer."

Dana laughed. "As far as I'm concerned, Olivia made everything right again the moment she stepped into the examination room. However, Catherine felt a little differently. I wasn't sure who she wanted to kill first, Olivia or Dr. Snyder."

"Olivia told me. She feels really bad about the way things ended today with her and Catherine. She hopes to have a chance to talk to her, once the dust settles."

Dana crossed her legs and stretched her arm across the back of the couch. "That could be wishful thinking. You should have seen them together, Ruth. There were murderous sparks flying all over the place. It's amazing we all walked away from that unscathed."

Ruth laughed. "Do you think there could be something there between Catherine and Olivia?"

"That's a lovely thought, but I don't think so. The last person I could imagine Catherine getting involved with would be a surgical oncologist."

"What a shame. We could each find a partner for someone we love in one little match-making venture."

Dana smiled. "After what I saw today, that's highly improbable. How are you, Ruth? You must be exhausted after everything you've been through today."

"I'm tired. I'll make sure my mom's settled for the night then I'm heading to her house to get some sleep. It's been a stressful day for you too. But I wanted to congratulate you on your clean mammogram and breast exam. It's been five years now, Dana. You can stop taking your Tamoxifen."

Dana skimmed her fingertips across the seam in the plush suede. "I needed to hear it from you before I felt totally comfortable with it."

"You have my permission to stop taking your meds. You've made it to five years without recurrence, Dana. I'm so happy for you."

"Thank you. When I dreamed of achieving this milestone I promised myself I'd toss my remaining pills out to sea. Now that the time is here I'm terrified to let them go."

"I know. It's like letting go of a trusted friend."

Dana anchored her foot on the antique black cherry coffee table. "I couldn't have done it without you, Dr. Ratcliff."

"I'm thrilled to have been there with you every step of the way, Dana. I'm even more thrilled to be considered a friend.

I'd like the opportunity to celebrate your five-year mark with you. I'd also like to find a way to make it up to you for what you went through today."

"I rather do enjoy dinner with you."

"Sounds wonderful. It's a date. I should get going, unfortunately. But I can't tell you how much hearing your voice has calmed me."

"It was great talking to you, Ruth. Can I call you tomorrow to check on both of you?"

"I'd like that."

"Good night, Ruth. Take care of yourself and your mother. Know that you're both in my prayers."

"Thanks, Dana. That means a lot to me. Good-bye, my friend."

Dana clicked off her phone and held it to her chest. "Good-bye, my friend."

Five

OLIVIA SLICED THROUGH THE WATER of their indoor lap pool at a breakneck pace. She reached the end and executed a perfect underwater turn and headed in the opposite direction. Olivia saw the feet dangling in the shallow end and slowed her frantic pace. She reached for the edge of the pool beside Echo's legs and surfaced. She gasped her next breath and pulled her goggles off her face and placed them on the deck. Olivia dunked herself to get the hair out of her eyes and wiped at the water on her face. She swiftly hauled herself out of the pool and sat beside Echo.

Echo handed her a plush pink towel. "You look like a woman hell bent on beating the water into a foam rather than swimming in it."

Olivia lifted her face from the towel. "It's been quite a day. Is Zoë asleep?"

"She's been sound asleep since nine. I was working on my paper about women and heart disease when I heard you come in. I wanted to make sure you were okay." Echo grabbed a bag of pretzels and held them before Olivia. "Want a pretzel? They always make the world a better place."

Olivia looked down at the bag before her and laughed. "No thanks, Echo. That's not going to fix what ails me."

"What about some of my awesome veggie stir-fry? We were kind enough to save you some. Are you hungry?"

"Sorry I missed dinner, Echo. I'm really not very hungry."

Echo gasped. "Okay, now I know you had a really bad day. You never lose your appetite."

Olivia rubbed her weary eyes then gently massaged her own temples. "It's just one of those days you wish you could do all over again. Especially the lecture."

"The lecture was great. Even the question from Catherine O'Grady gave the audience something to think about." Echo looked closely at her friend. "You're upset about Catherine O'Grady, aren't you?"

"She didn't make my day any easier."

"How do you even know her? Have you been to her bookstore?"

"No. I didn't know she existed before today. She's the daughter of one of Ruth's patients. She bashed me during their appointment today, then did it again at the lecture."

"You must care about this total stranger, to let her upset you so much."

Olivia rose to her feet and reached for the white terry-cloth robe draped across the lounge chair. "What I care about right now is getting some sleep." She slipped her arms into the sleeves. "It's late, Echo. We should get to bed. I can only pray that tomorrow will be a better day."

Echo slipped out of the water and dried off her legs. Olivia held the French doors open for her and they entered the kitchen. Olivia felt so grateful for this spacious house, the way it welcomed her home from a hard day, the love and support she felt here from Zoë and Echo. The three of them had met in college and lived together ever since, except for the years she and Echo completed their fellowships in different parts of the country.

Echo put away the pretzels and they climbed the stairs together, stopping in the entranceway of Olivia's wing. Echo touched Olivia's arm. "I'm sorry you have so much to deal with right now, Olivia. Maybe there's a message in this clash with you and Catherine O'Grady."

"The message I'm getting is to run as fast and far as I can."

Echo laughed. "That was obviously your intent in the pool tonight. Good night, Olivia."

"Good night, Echo. I'll see you in the morning."

Olivia waved as she headed down the long hall to her bedroom. She opened the door, swore, and placed her hand over her racing heart. The gray slacks she'd left draped across her bed haphazardly bounced up and down on the floor like half a human being break-dancing to its own rhythm.

"That's it. You guys are dead." Abbott scooted out of the bottom of one leg while Costello dashed out the waist. They looked back at Olivia with their dark beady eyes then raced for the bathroom.

Six

OLIVIA HURRIED DOWN THE STAIRS and stopped to leave her knapsack in the front foyer. She zipped up her sweatshirt then peered into the huge sun-filled kitchen. The light pine cupboards and marble countertops gave warmth to the spaciousness.

Zoë stood at the island counter in the center of the kitchen. She was dressed in a beautiful white knit blouse and long teal beaded silk skirt that accentuated her girlish beauty and short dark hair. She sipped on a glass of orange juice as she laughed at something at her feet.

Olivia followed a rustling noise to the floor in front of the fridge. She gasped and stepped back as a cereal box flipped at her feet and slid away. Abbott shot from the box and joined Costello in front of the fridge. Costello pulled the magnetic letter L from the door and ran for the cereal box, dropping it inside. Abbott added the letter O, flipped around in the box, then scampered back to retrieve another letter.

Zoë burst into laughter. "Aren't they precious?"

"Hardly. They'll be the death of me. I wondered what happened to them when I saw their cage empty this morning."

"Echo brought them down to let them run around. They're so adorable."

"They're a menace to my state of mind." Olivia wrapped her arms around Zoë. "Good morning."

Zoë beamed her beautiful smile. "Good morning, Olivia. How did you sleep?"

Olivia pressed her hand to Zoë's round tummy. "I could use another couple of hours, but I need a hike even more. How about you?"

"I slept great. Sorry I didn't wait up for you. I was beat."

Olivia looked around the kitchen. "Where's Echo?"

"She got paged several times last night about one of her patients. She had him transferred into the coronary care unit and wanted to head out early to check on him." She poured Olivia a glass of orange juice. "Sorry things were rough between you and Catherine O'Grady yesterday. She seems like such a sweet person."

Olivia took a deep drink of her orange juice. "For a sweet person she's certainly bent and determined to test my spirit."

Zoë placed a bowl of Special K in front of Olivia and smiled mischievously. "Echo thinks you're attracted to her."

"Zoë, I barely know her."

"You know she's gay, don't you?"

Olivia dropped back in her chair. A tight ball of heat swirled in her belly as she wondered if that was why she felt a connection to Catherine. She'd tossed and turned with her thoughts last night, wondering how she could find a way to see Dana O'Grady's daughter again. "How would I know that?"

"Actually, I don't know for sure, but she's got this wonderful bookstore, and a lot of the gay community goes there, and that's what I've heard."

Zoë slipped into her seat and poured milk on her cereal. She wanted so badly to see Olivia in a loving relationship. For years Olivia had insisted she didn't have time for romance. Her work was really important to her, and that was where she needed to put her time. She insisted that Zoë and Echo were her family, and she was willing to accept being single unless someone extraordinary crossed her path.

Zoë bit into a lush strawberry. "You never know, Olivia. Catherine O'Grady could turn out to be a lovely challenge."

Olivia stared at her. "Are you kidding? Catherine and I are on very shaky ground."

"You haven't been in an earthquake in a while."

Olivia rolled her eyes. They finished their cereal and rose with their empty bowls and glasses. Zoë rinsed the dishes and placed them into the dishwasher.

Olivia scooped Abbott and Costello off the floor and nestled them in her arms. Their lithe, serpentine bodies moved fluidly as Abbott slinked along Olivia's arm and nipped at the shiny buckle of her watch. Costello stretched to investigate her gold-loop earrings. "These two are forever looking for something shiny to steal."

"They sure are. Echo couldn't find her Mont Blanc pen this morning. She said if it doesn't show up she's going to tell Ruth she owes her one for her birthday."

Olivia rubbed her thumb along Abbott's face, feeling the smoothness of his short, caramel-colored fur. "Come on, you two kleptomaniacs. I'm putting you back in your cage."

"That's a good idea. The workmen are coming to start the remodeling work on our bathroom. We're really lucky they were willing to come on a Saturday." Zoë dried her hands on the hand towel. "Ruth would kill us if anything happened to her little darlings."

"Yeah, and I don't think I can handle having another woman pissed at me."

Zoë caressed Abbott's face. "You have to admit, Olivia. They're so cute and playful."

"They weren't so cute when they climbed into my pants and started bouncing all over my bedroom floor last night. I just about had a heart attack."

Zoë burst into laughter. "Oh, Olivia. That must have been a sight. Not something you ever imagined climbing into your pants."

Olivia laughed. "No, certainly not what my dreams are made of."

Seven

DANA SET THE STACK of computer books down on the customer-service desk and grabbed the phone. Catherine had gone to the hospital to deliver a box of used romance novels for the volunteers to hand out to patients. "Thank you for calling Cocoa Cream. This is Dana. How may I help you?"

"You can begin by telling me your daughter doesn't hate me."

Dana's laughter filled the phone line as she slipped onto the nearest stool. "My daughter couldn't hate anyone. How are you, Olivia?"

"Not too bad, considering the rodents in my home and the workload at the hospital. Except for a quick hike Saturday morning I spent most of my weekend with patients. Dana, tell me honestly. Do you think Catherine would be willing to talk to me? I'm not comfortable with how we left things on Friday."

Dana was a little surprised by the question. She also felt pleased. She wondered if Ruth might be right about Catherine and Olivia's feelings for each other, or at least Olivia's feelings for Catherine.

"I think she'd be more than willing to talk to you, Olivia. And I think I know where you'll find her."

Olivia cautiously walked through the open doorway, feeling the slight resistance she always felt entering a place of worship. The front wall of mirrors reflected back the multitude of lit candles dancing to a rhythm of their own. A huge wooden cross adorned the area behind the alter with a white sheer fabric draped over its arms. The setting sun streamed through the floor-to-ceiling stained-glass windows illuminating the interior in greens and blues. Then she saw the figure in the first pew.

Catherine was alone, kneeling with her head bowed against her entwined hands. The stark light shone off her blond highlights and enveloped her slim frame. Olivia felt a peculiar tension in her chest as she absorbed Catherine's distress.

She heard Catherine praying softly and felt like an intruder. Her first impulse was to run. Instead she felt herself pulled to this woman's raw emotions. She walked to the front of the chapel and slipped into a pew a safe distance away across the aisle. Catherine's thick dark eyelashes rested softly against her olive complexion. Her small nose and full, soft lips were silhouetted by the flickering candlelight. An exquisite teardrop diamond twinkled on her earlobe, and tears glistened on her cheeks. She looked up. They stared for a few seconds before Catherine dug into her purse for a tissue.

Olivia nervously cleared her throat. "Are you okay?"

Catherine dried her eyes. "I'm fine. This place tends to do this to me." She rose from the pew and stepped into the aisle. "I'm sure you came to have a moment to yourself. I'll leave you alone."

"I've actually never been in the hospital chapel. Religion isn't my strong suit. But your mother said I'd find you here."

"My mother?"

"Yes. I called Cocoa Cream looking for you. Do you have a few minutes to talk?"

Catherine looked down. "We don't seem to do that very well, Dr. Carrington."

"I know. I was hoping we could change that."

Catherine turned in the aisle to face her. "Why?"

Olivia stretched her arm across the back of the pew. "Because I can't get you off my mind, Ms. O'Grady. We may never see each other again after today, but for some reason it matters to me that I clear the air with you."

Catherine was taken aback. She'd been trying all weekend to shake the physical draw she felt toward Olivia Carrington. Was the feeling mutual?

She slid tentatively into the end of the pew and crossed her legs. Olivia's flowing dark hair framed her face beautifully as the light highlighted her high cheekbones and full lips. She was immaculately dressed in a black turtleneck and charcoal plaid slacks beneath her pristine white lab coat.

"You have my undivided attention."

Olivia hesitated, struggling to find the right words. "I wanted to acknowledge that you're right," she said finally. "Every woman does deserve access to all the treatments available. I have some information on complementary therapies I wanted to offer you, as well as the current articles on alternative therapies to have on hand for your customers." Catherine felt her defenses go back up. Was this why Olivia couldn't get her off her mind, because of their argument on Friday? Because of her professional pride?

"I appreciate that."

They sat for a moment awkwardly. She took a breath. "I can't imagine doing the work you do, Olivia. What happened in your life that made you choose this career path?"

"My maternal grandmother died of breast cancer when I was fourteen. I was very close to her and it tore me apart to see the way she suffered. I promised her before she died that I would become a doctor and make things better for women diagnosed with breast cancer. I've worked very hard to keep that promise to her."

Catherine's heart went out to Olivia. She wished losing a loved one to cancer wasn't something they shared. "I'm sure your grandmother is very proud of you."

"She better be. I'm busting my butt every day for her."

Catherine smiled. "Do you worry about your mother and yourself because of your grandmother's cancer history?"

"My mammograms have all been clean. I have so many patients to worry about that I don't have time to dwell on my own family history. As for my mother, I gave up worrying about her years ago."

Catherine turned in the pew to face her directly. "What do you mean?"

"My mom and I aren't very close."

"I'm so sorry. I don't know how I'd survive without my mother."

"I envy the closeness you have with Dana. The only good thing about what happened with my mother is how close it brought me to my dad, Brady. He's tremendous. And so is his partner, Austin. But that's another story for another time."

Catherine laughed. "It sounds like a good one."

"It certainly made for some interesting dinnertime discussions on sexuality, especially when I was a teenager discovering my own path."

"I bet they were very supportive when you told them you were attracted to women."

Olivia leaned back slightly. "Am I that obvious?"

Catherine smiled. "No, you could never be a poster girl for the typical lesbian. But you did set off my gaydar." She paused. "Did I set off yours?"

"Not in the slightest. I would never have known you were a lesbian. I have a very poor sense of picking out lesbians. But I had informants, my housemates Echo and Zoë. They were at the lecture yesterday. They've been to your bookstore."

"The pregnant couple? I was wondering how you knew them."

"We all met in college. We've lived together ever since, except the years Echo and I went our separate ways for our fellowships. Echo's a cardiologist and did her fellowship in Boston. Zoë's an amazing financial advisor. When we all landed back here in San Diego, we told Brady what we would all want in a dream home and he built it for us in Hillcrest. It's a monstrosity of a house, but it's home. It was his gift to all of us." Olivia traced the seam on her slacks. "I love those two. They're just like sisters to me."

"They obviously care very much for you. I've noticed them in the bookstore. They make such a beautiful couple."

"They truly are. They met when they were sixteen. They're high school sweethearts and they're going to celebrate their sixteenth anniversary this summer."

"Wow. And now a baby."

"They've been talking about having a baby for years and they finally went ahead with their plans. Zoë's due in nine weeks."

"They should write a book about their success. I would buy it for the bookstore. Heck, I'd like to know their secret myself."

"Genuine love and respect. That's what they tell people is their secret. Somehow I think great sex fits into that recipe somewhere as well. They're always very open about that."

"Good for them." Catherine took a breath. "I'm really glad you came looking for me, Olivia."

Olivia slid closer in the pew. "Why were you crying when I first walked in?"

Catherine stared down at her hands and balled the tissue in her fist. "I always come here to talk to my dad. I really miss him."

Olivia reached over and gently squeezed her shoulder. That simple touch filled Catherine with a heat that flowed to places that had been untouched in two years. "I'm sorry about your dad. I'm sorry you've had to deal with your mother's breast cancer as well. I wish I could ease the worry you feel about your own health."

Catherine struggled against the tears threatening to spill. "Well, you know how they say what won't kill you will make you a better person. That seems to hold true in my family."

Olivia watched Catherine carefully. "Thank you for staying and talking to me. I hate to leave, but I've got a few patients I still need to see this evening."

"Thank you for coming to find me."

Olivia slipped into the aisle. "Can I walk you out?"

"I think I'll stay for a few minutes. I'd like to light some candles before I go."

"Make sure you light a candle for all those good doctors battling the evils of cancer."

"I will."

Olivia smiled and headed out the door. Catherine leaned back and sighed heavily. "And I'll light a candle for you, Dr. Olivia Carrington. I can only pray it will help me to understand why you walked into my life."

Eight

OLIVIA BID HER RESIDENTS good night. It had been yet another chaotic day, and she felt the headache tugging at her temples. Ruth had been gone five full days now, and she was really feeling her absence.

She headed down the hall and checked her patient list one final time. She walked through the glass automatic doors and headed out into the cool evening air, stopping to listen to the rustling sound of the wind toying with the palm fronds. It was a beautiful March evening, as she admired the hilly expanse of San Diego sprawled below. Olivia wished she could be part of the traffic moving swiftly along Interstate 5. To the west, the brilliant orange sun was about to set into the Pacific Ocean. How her tired feet would love to feel that damp cool sand right now.

She inhaled deeply and headed across the walkway connecting the hospital to the adjacent medical building. She tucked her patient list into the pocket of her lab coat and squeezed her tired neck. It was already six-thirty; she had at least a couple of hours of desk work ahead of her and suddenly felt exhausted.

Stepping into an empty elevator, she leaned her head back against the cool wood paneling, closing her eyes for a moment before the elevator chimed its arrival at the fifth floor.

She stepped off the elevator and unlocked the door to their office suite. The silence inside was blissful.

She headed into her office, grabbed a bottle of water from the bar fridge, and sunk into her cherry-red executive leather chair. She uncapped the bottle and took a deep swallow, then eyed the cordless phone on her desk. She'd resisted contacting Catherine for more than twenty-four hours. Surely that was enough. She reached for the phone.

"Thank you for calling Cocoa Cream. This is Catherine, how may I help you?"

"I was wondering if you carried the book *How To Win Friends and Influence People* by Dale Carnegie?"

Catherine laughed. "We sure do. It's a classic. Shall I reserve one for you, Dr. Carrington?"

"Please. I thought I'd pick up some tips on how to draw people to me, rather than at me."

"In that case, I'll have it delivered overnight." They both laughed. "How was your day, Olivia?"

"It was busy. I performed mastectomies on three women. I just finished checking on them and I'm happy to say that they're all recovering comfortably."

Catherine suddenly felt tense. She'd been pleased to hear Olivia's voice, but instantly felt herself withdraw when the topic shifted to cancer. "You sound tired."

"I'm beat. I just landed in my office. Tell me about your day at Cocoa Cream."

"It was chaotically busy, though I think I prefer our kind of chaos to yours. We had a group of twenty-five third graders come in this afternoon as part of a Promote Reading Program. A local children's author talked to them and read from her current book. And for the grand finale they watched a puppet show while we gave them drinks and snacks."

"And here I thought you just had a coffee shop and bookstore. How come I never got to go on any cool school trips like that when I was in the third grade?"

"Did you even attend the third grade or did you just go from diapers to high school?"

"If I'd been fortunate enough to discover a bookstore like yours at that young impressionable age I just might have. However, I was just an average student. I went through each grade like every other normal kid and studied my brains out to get where I am today."

"I'd have to see your report cards and survey your roommates to believe that, Olivia. An average student doesn't become a surgical oncologist at your age."

"Just like an average student doesn't run such a successful bookstore and coffee shop at your age."

"I'm thirty-five, Olivia. I was just very lucky to be able to purchase this place ten years ago with my parent's financial help. My mom and I both believe our success is equal parts Irish luck, hard-working employees, and great location."

"I don't doubt any of that. But somehow I think the women behind Cocoa Cream are the keys to its success. Those are the thoughts of a woman a year wiser than you."

"Well then, old wise one, you're just going to have to step inside our doors and see if that statement's true."

"I'd love that."

"Are you going to be able to head home soon?"

"Probably in a couple of hours. I have teaching rounds with the residents tomorrow so I need to finish preparing some case studies for them. We'll be talking about the indications for mastectomies versus lumpectomies."

Olivia was aware of the silence on the other end of the line. "Sounds very interesting," Catherine said finally.

"You're a terrible liar, Catherine. And I mean that as a compliment. Obviously what you've been through with your parents has left you deeply scared. Can I give you my cell phone number? I'd like to be there for you if you just need to talk."

"It's not that easy, Olivia. But I do appreciate your kindness."

"I don't sense that anything is easy about you, Catherine. Do you have a pen handy?"

"I do."

Catherine scribbled down Olivia's cell phone number, feeling a flush of excitement in spite of herself.

"I should go so I can get my work done," Olivia said. "Good night, Catherine."

"Good-bye, Olivia."

Catherine hung up the phone and sat for a moment with her eyes closed.

"What was that all about?"

Catherine swiveled in her chair. "Laura, you scared me. I didn't see you standing there."

"That was obvious from the outset of your conversation. What did Dr. Olivia Carrington want?"

"I've been trying to figure that out since I met her." She leaned across the counter toward her friend. "She fascinates me and she scares me. She epitomizes the type of person I don't want in my life. I run from cancer and Olivia lives and breathes it. I strive to live a modest life and I think she enjoys living on a grander scale. Those things set off red flags and I still find I'm replaying our conversations in my head over and over again. I just can't seem to get her off my mind."

Laura looked concerned. "It seems to me that the two of you clash more than you connect. Promise me that you'll be careful."

"I'm always careful, Laura. Mostly I want to keep her as a friend, and I'm hoping that's what she's looking for, too. I just wish she wasn't so damn gorgeous."

"If you want my opinion, I'd say Dr. Olivia Carrington is looking for more than friendship, and my best friend is the one who's likely to get hurt." Laura took a breath and glanced over her shoulder. "The last time I checked, the kids were sprawled in beanbags in the children's section with their dad. Let's go round them up and get out of here."

Catherine rose from her chair. "You're right. It's time to go home."

Catherine and Laura walked around the huge plaster Cat in the Hat and into the children's section. Catherine stopped to pick up a fallen book. Laura knelt down behind Kevin and wrapped her arms around him. He had Amanda and Sean nestled in each arm and Harry Potter perched in his lap. He leaned back to give Laura a smacking kiss then continued reading.

Catherine felt a familiar tug in her gut every time she saw them together. She envied what Laura had and longed for a family of her own. She could only dream and hope that one day she could fill that void. She slipped the book back on the shelf and took Amanda's outstretched hand.

Nine

CATHERINE FINISHED RESTOCKING the Books on CD section and pushed her metal cart toward the storage room.

Dana emerged from the Cooking, Food, & Wine section. "If you're heading back to the office can you take this book with you? The cover's torn. I'll send it back to the publisher."

Catherine placed the book on her cart. "Consider it done. Is it lunchtime yet?"

"Sure feels like it. Give me fifteen minutes to finish straightening out this section and I'll meet you in the office."

"That's a date."

Catherine passed the Women's Health aisle and saw an elderly woman holding a book in each hand with a perplexed look on her face. She parked the cart at the end of the aisle and carefully approached. The woman was reading the back cover of one of the books. "Are you finding everything you need?" Catherine asked.

The woman looked over her bifocals at Catherine's name badge and smiled. "Actually, I never expected to find so many books on breast cancer. I'm a little overwhelmed by your selection."

"I know what you mean. I'm continually shocked by the number of books written on the subject." Feeling both drawn to this lovely woman and wanting to run, Catherine looked at the books the woman held. She touched the one in her right hand. *"Dr. Susan Love's Breast Book* is one of the best. I read it cover to cover when my mother was diagnosed five years ago. It was an excellent reference guide."

"Is your mother all right?"

"She's terrific. She has to be, because I could never run this bookstore without her. She had a lumpectomy and radiation therapy. We feel very thankful at how well she's done." Catherine extended her hand. "I'm Catherine. I own this blessed pile of books you're trying to decide on."

The elderly lady slipped the books back on the shelf and took Catherine's hand. "Hello, Catherine. I'm Emma. I'm so glad to hear your mother's well."

"She's right over there. Why don't I introduce you?" Catherine signaled Dana to come over.

"Emma, this is my mother, Dana O'Grady."

"Hello, Dana. It's a pleasure to meet you. Catherine was telling me about your breast cancer. I'm so glad to hear you're well. I fought this disease fifteen years ago, and I'm afraid I've been diagnosed again."

Catherine swallowed hard as she saw the fear and disbelief in the woman's moist eyes.

Dana reached out and took her hand. "I'm so sorry."

The phone rang at the customer-service desk. Catherine quickly looked from Emma to her mother. "Excuse me while I answer that."

Emma followed Catherine's path. "I've made her uncomfortable. I'm sorry."

"Please don't be. My breast cancer was really hard on Catherine. Your story brings back all her fears and heartache."

"I often wondered what it would be like to have a daughter with me at a time like this. I have four sons and this sort of thing is very hard for the boys to deal with."

"I can only imagine. But tell me about your diagnosis."

Dana listened compassionately as Emma recounted her story. She'd had a mastectomy fifteen years before. Her husband had been wonderfully supportive, but he'd recently passed away. Now she'd been diagnosed with a tumor in her remaining breast.

"The worst part is that my pathetic young doctor thinks I'm too old to operate on. I may be seventy years old, but I'm not dead. I have no other medical problems besides my achy old bones. I take care of myself. I do all my own shopping and chores. I walk my dog, Millie, five miles a day. I told that brainless doctor he grossly underestimated me if he planned to limit my options because of my age and stormed out of his office." She shook her head. "The problem is, I don't know what to do next. I decided today to come here to do some reading, but I don't know where to begin. What I do know is I beat this once, and I can beat it again."

Dana squeezed her shoulder. "Good girl. I think the best place for you to start is to get yourself another doctor."

"Unfortunately, the doctor I had fifteen years ago retired. I really liked him. This new one is still wet behind the ears and a very poor listener. I sense these young doctors are adverse to risk and failure."

"The only failure is in not trying, not fighting, and not having the opportunity to win. You already have a winning attitude. We just need to find you the right doctor who'll fight along with you. My surgical oncologist is wonderful. She works out of the Cancer Center at University Hospital.

Why don't we see if we can get you an appointment with her or her partner?"

"Do you think they would see me?"

"Yes, I do. They both have years of experience, they're good listeners, and they're fighters. Just like you. Let's go into the office and make that call."

Dana sat close by as Emma articulately explained her story to the receptionist, silently praying that Ruth or Olivia would be able to help this lovely woman. Emma answered a series of questions and jotted some information on a scratch pad.

She hung up and turned to Dana, blinking as the tears filled her eyes. "I have an appointment next week with Dr. Olivia Carrington. They had a cancellation, so the receptionist fit me in."

Dana handed her a tissue from the desk. "That's wonderful. Now you can begin to wage your winning battle."

Emma reached for Dana's hand. "I knew I needed to come here, but I didn't know why. Now I know. I was guided."

Dana found Catherine reorganizing the announcement board. "Now you must really be ready for lunch."

"I'm starving." Catherine looked over her mother's shoulder and saw Emma sipping a cup of coffee and leafing through Dr. Susan Love's book. She felt drawn to this woman in a way she hadn't anticipated. "How's Emma?"

"She's such a sweetheart. She has an appointment with Olivia next week."

Catherine blinked. "She does? That's fantastic. I hope Olivia can help her."

"I hope so, too. Emma promised she'd come back and let me know how she's doing. Now, lets go get something to eat."

"I didn't mean to make such a hasty exit."

"I know."

"Emma probably thinks I'm weak."

"Emma completely understands how you feel."

"I wish I could help like you do, Mom, rather than trying to find the nearest escape route."

"Your help is invaluable, baby. Emma bought the book you recommended. Combine that with her appointment with Olivia, and she'll walk out of this bookstore a changed woman."

Ten

THE POSTMAN WOVE HIS WAY among the crowded tables in the coffee shop at four o'clock, right on schedule. He waved at Catherine with a handful of mail and gave her his usual endearing smile. "Top of the afternoon to you, Ms. Catherine."

"Top of the afternoon to you, Tom. When did a die-hard Texan become so Irish?"

He placed a stack of mail on the counter and dug into his huge shoulder bag. "All these lovely St. Patrick's Day decorations bring out the best Irish in me." He pulled three packages out and handed them to Catherine. "Where's your lovely mother this bright and beautiful Thursday?"

"She headed out to run some errands." Catherine glanced at the packages. Her heart jumped as she noticed that one of them was addressed to her, from Olivia Carrington.

"Lovely as a rose, your mother is. I've been trying for years to get her to have dinner with me but she won't have any of it. But I'm not giving up. Someday she'll see what a great catch a Texas cowboy can be."

Catherine smiled. "Tom, you've been married and divorced four times. I think your track record has you hog-tied in my mother's eyes."

"Maybe it's her I've been looking for my whole life."

"I hate to disappoint you, but my mother has said my father was the only man for her."

Tom heaved the bin of outgoing mail onto his big shoulder. "How am I supposed to compete with that?"

"You're not. Just be her friend, and she'll adore you for it."

"All I can say is your father was one very lucky man for having both of you."

"Actually, Tom, we were the lucky ones."

"I believe that to be true. See you tomorrow, Ms. Catherine."

Catherine slipped into her office and tore open the package from Olivia. She found a stack of articles inside, stapled together with a note on pale yellow paper. Secured to the top right-hand corner of the note was a silver-plated and enameled pink-ribbon tack pin. Scrolled across the ribbon was *Find a Cure*. Catherine set the pin against the small treasure chest on her desk and read the note, feeling her excitement over the package ebb.

Dear Catherine,

    I thought you might find these articles interesting. They explain the current breakthroughs in cancer research, the focus of today's research goals, and how money is spent on prevention, early detection, treatment, and research. The best article is the last one discussing the success of current breast cancer therapies. I wanted you to see how many people are working hard to prove the power and success of Western medicine. The enemy is working hard to win you over.

    I was given a bunch of those breast cancer tack pins by one of our drug representatives. I thought you could put it

in your office and every day it would remind you that so
many people are truly working hard to find a cure.

Take care of yourself, Catherine. Please give me a call
when you have a spare moment.

Warmly,
Olivia

Catherine took a deep breath. It distressed her how easily distracted she was by thoughts of Olivia. She felt challenged by her intelligence and insight, warmed by her sense of humor and charm. But their lives were so different, so contradictory. Contradictions that could never be overcome.

She flipped through the articles. She was deeply grateful this research was being done, and that women like Emma had a chance to fight their cancer because of it. She admired Olivia for immersing her life in the world of medicine. A world she needed to shield herself from to protect her sanity.

She was about to set the articles aside when she noticed a pink letter-size envelope at the bottom of the stack. Curious, she opened it, unfolding a copy of Olivia's third-grade report card. She burst into laughter as she scanned down the straight A's and read the teacher's comments at the bottom of the page.

She sat for a moment, pulled in two directions, then reached for her cell phone and dialed Olivia's cell number. A fluttering sensation tingled her skin.

"This is Dr. Carrington."

"Did I catch you at a good time, Olivia?"

"Catherine! Your timing is perfect. I'm just heading back to my office."

Catherine picked up the tack pin and held it gently in the palm of her hand. "Thank you for the breast-cancer pin."

"It's just something to remind you of the people you can't see who are fighting hard against that evil cancer you also can't see."

"I have faith in the people and the process, Olivia. Some days my fear dims my faith."

"I can understand that, with your family history. I just hope you'll give me the opportunity to strengthen your faith and dim your fear."

They were silent for a moment. Catherine reached for the report card. "I now have evidence that you actually attended the third grade."

"See, and you doubted me."

"I won't make that mistake again. The best part is your teacher's comments at the bottom of the page. 'Olivia is a pleasure to have as a student. She works very hard at her studies and actively participates in class. She listens well and is eager to learn. She plays very well with the girls in the class but seems to have an intolerance for the boys.'" Catherine laughed. "Olivia, you were outed by your third-grade teacher."

"And I adored that teacher. I can't believe she did that to me at such a young impressionable age."

"It's amazing that you're so well adjusted after a report card like that."

They laughed together as Catherine placed the report card down on her desk. "How does the rest of your day look?"

"I just walked into my office. I have five patients here waiting to see me and then I have to do my rounds in the hospital before I can go home. I'm being reminded of my residency days when the hospital was the only home I knew."

"So much for trying to maintain your sanity with a life outside of work."

"My life outside of work has been seriously lacking for a long time."

"I should let you go, then."

"Thank you so much for calling, Catherine. It was the highlight of my day." Olivia's voice was warm and sincere. Once again, Catherine's heart lurched, as much as she wished it wouldn't.

"I hope the rest of your day goes well, Olivia, and that you get home before eleven o'clock."

"The chances of that happening are pretty slim. Good-bye, Catherine. I'll talk to you soon."

"Good-bye, Olivia." Catherine clicked off the phone, laid her head back against her chair, and closed her eyes. "What am I going to do with you, Dr. Olivia Carrington?"

Eleven

CATHERINE SET HER KETTLE to boil and looked around her small kitchen. She loved its homey feeling. She'd bought this old 1950s house because of its charm and worked hard to restore it, preserving the original style and woodwork. She'd never been a fan of new and ostentatious homes. She remembered Olivia speaking of her "monstrosity of a house," and couldn't imagine her appreciating this modest one.

The kettle's whistle startled her from her thoughts. She filled her bone-china teacup and headed for her favorite over-stuffed chair, carefully sipping the hot tea as she curled her legs beneath her. She stared into the crackling fire and watched the flames lick at the maple logs as her favorite Celtic Sisters CD played low in the background.

Catherine was bothered by the excitement she'd felt when she spoke to Olivia. She would have to call upon her sense of self-preservation; there was simply no way the two of them could be involved, and she was starting to agree with Laura that Olivia hoped for involvement. Sipping her tea, she resolved to stand firm, to stop herself from being drawn in any further by Dr. Olivia Carrington.

The musical tune of her cell phone startled her from her thoughts. She looked over at the mantel clock and could think of only one person who would be calling her at ten-thirty at night. A glance at the display on her cell phone confirmed the thought.

"Hello, Dr. Carrington. Please tell me you're home."

Olivia laughed. "I'm about two minutes from home. I know it's late, Catherine. I hope I didn't wake you."

"Not at all. I'm curled up in my favorite chair enjoying a fire and a cup of green tea."

"That sounds lovely. I wanted to thank you and your mother for referring Emma to me yesterday. The office staff told me about her call today before I left. I hope we can help her."

"I hope so too, Olivia. She's a fighter. I can't believe that a physician would look at a woman's age and make a plan of care without taking the person into consideration."

"Age is only one factor, and certainly never a deciding factor. I'll see what we can do for Emma when she comes in next week. I promise you that I'll give her my best."

"I don't doubt that for a moment, Olivia." Catherine heard a car door slam. "How was the rest of your evening?"

"The office appointments went smoothly. Then I spent some time with a patient I did a mastectomy on yesterday, who I admitted into the ICU."

Catherine hesitated. "How's she doing?"

"Not as well as I'd hoped. I'm afraid she'll develop pneumonia if we don't control her pain better so she can deep breathe. And I'm worried about her daughter."

"Why?"

"She's having a real hard time dealing with her mother's diagnosis and surgery. She's only twenty-five. Her mother's only forty-eight. When I first met her in my office she seemed distant, timid, and skittish. She didn't have many questions. Now I think it's just that she's terrified of what's going on."

"I can understand how she feels."

"I know you can. I'd like to talk with your mom about her. I'm hoping she can help me with this family."

Catherine hugged a pillow tight to her chest. "I'm sure she'll be happy to help. Are you home now, Olivia?"

"I just got here. I'm grabbing a glass of orange juice, and then I plan to sit on our back deck to enjoy the full moon and you. What time did you finally leave the bookstore?"

"I didn't get out of there till seven o'clock. We have an all-male reading group that meets at the bookstore every Thursday. The average age of these guys is seventy, and you wouldn't know it by their behavior. They were supposed to be discussing *Wuthering Heights* when they got into a heated discussion about the war in Afghanistan. My mom went over and told them they were behaving worse than the group of third graders we had in yesterday. She was the perfect distraction for them. They totally lost their train of thought and started flirting with her. I believe she came away with two marriage proposals and a promise to be more civil."

"I'm not surprised. Your mother's an incredible woman. I'm sure any one of those men would jump at the opportunity to win her affection."

Catherine was aware of how much she enjoyed talking to Olivia, as long as the subject wasn't a difficult one. "She's too young for them, and she isn't interested in dating. She was so devoted to my father that I don't think she even sees the way those men look at her."

"That's a shame, because I sense your mother has so much to offer in a relationship."

"I agree with you, but it would take an incredible person to break through her walls."

"Did your parents meet in Ireland or were they already in the U.S.?"

"Both sets of my grandparents immigrated to the U.S. shortly after they were married. So my parents are second-generation immigrants. They met when my mother hired my father to do the accounts for her real-estate agency. As the story goes, it was love at first sight." Catherine leaned her head back against her chair. "I'd like to see her share a relationship with someone special again, but it would be really strange to see her with anyone other than my father."

"I understand that."

"I guess you do. You would never have imagined your father falling in love with another man."

"No, that wasn't exactly what I'd envisioned for him. Hey, who knows, your mom might be holding out for the right woman."

Catherine laughed. "Now, that I'd love to see."

"I love to hear you laugh, Catherine. I really enjoy you." The silence stretched for a few long seconds. "Did I lose you?"

"No."

"What just happened?"

"Just before you called I was wondering how I'm going to keep you at a safe distance."

"Obviously you have reasons for wanting to keep me at a safe distance."

"Several."

"Care to share them with me?"

"Nope."

"How fair is that?"

Catherine stared into the crackling fire. "Life isn't always fair, Olivia. I see our lives as being very different. There are things about you that make me feel uncomfortable. But I can't seem to get you off my mind or stop myself from wondering when we'll talk again. I know that sounds crazy."

"It *is* crazy. You're just getting to know me, Catherine. Don't pass judgment till you've seen the whole picture. You've barely scratched the surface. I know my career makes you feel very uncomfortable. Let me help you overcome your fear."

"That's not possible, Olivia."

"I'm a pretty good judge of people, Catherine, and you never struck me as being so rigid. I won't apologize for my career. I love what I do. As for whatever else there is about my life that makes you uncomfortable, I can't help you with that if I don't know what's troubling you."

"It's just more of my fears and insecurities, Olivia. Just leave it at that." Catherine heard Olivia's exasperated sigh. "I've made you angry."

"What did you expect? Wouldn't you be pissed off if I told you our friendship was done at this point because of the little I knew about you? Well, I've got news for you. I care about you. I enjoy you. I had no idea this conversation would be our last."

"I don't want to lose your friendship, Olivia. I just need to keep you at a safe distance. I'm having a hard time understanding what you do to me and how I feel about you."

"I'm a little overwhelmed by my feelings for you as well, Catherine. But I'll give you all the distance you need. One thing I have very little of is time. I won't let you waste it. You know how to reach me. But I think you're making a mistake if you don't even try to figure out what we feel and what we could share."

Olivia clicked off her cell phone before Catherine could respond, and leaned forward in her patio chair. She stared into the circular gas fire pit, her tears blurring the blue-red flames dancing along the logs. She heard the sliding glass door open and turned to see Echo walk toward her.

Olivia wiped at her tears. "Echo, it's almost eleven. What're you doing up?"

"My very pregnant wife has a craving for a bowl of peas, which are cooking away in the microwave as we speak. She also claims to have a psychic connection to our daughter, who is requesting another slice of lemon meringue pie." Echo eased into the chair beside Olivia. "What's wrong?"

"I may have just talked to Catherine for the last time."

"What do you mean?"

"There seem to be things about me and my life that make her uncomfortable."

"Such as?"

"My career, for one. She wouldn't tell me what else. She chalks it up to fears and insecurities. How am I supposed to help her if she won't talk to me?"

Echo watched her friend carefully. "You care about her."

"Very much."

"What're you going to do about it?"

Olivia stared into the fire pit and watched the flames slither erratically around the logs. "Absolutely nothing. As of that phone conversation, we're done."

"I know you better than that, Olivia. When you care about someone, you don't give up so easily. How do you feel about her?"

Olivia looked into Echo's chocolate brown eyes. "She's beautiful, charming, fascinating, witty, and very bright. She stimulates my mind and sets me on fire. In essence, she scares me to death, and she dumped me before we could even get started. How's that for a kick in the pants?" Olivia shook her head. "I never thought I could go through another Jessica derailment. I feel like I've lost something special with Catherine, and I don't even know what we could have had."

Echo leaned closer. "Give it a few days. I don't believe for one minute this is any easier on Catherine than it is on you."

"Good. I hope her guts are twisted in knots, too."

"At the very least, don't throw away a friendship that obviously means something to you." Echo rose from her chair. "Come inside with me. I better get those peas and lemon meringue pie to my wife before my daughter gives her a psychic message that we're out here talking and not attending to their every dietary whim."

They stood together. Olivia touched Echo's shoulder. "Thanks."

"My pleasure. Be patient with Catherine. Obviously you overwhelm her as much as she overwhelms you."

"My patience with Catherine O'Grady is quickly vaporizing."

Echo laughed and guided Olivia to the sliding glass doors. "Oh, the trials and tribulations of lesbian attraction."

Twelve

CATHERINE WALKED CAREFULLY over the memorial stepping stones, reading the names and the inscriptions of loved ones who had died of cancer. The warm afternoon breeze embraced her as she stopped beneath the towering metal sculpture of a maple tree. Each brass leaf was engraved with a name and dates. Catherine wondered how her mother would feel about having her name and the dates of her life placed in this memorial cancer garden. Dana had told Catherine about this lovely garden on the hospital grounds several times. This was the first time she'd dared to venture through here. What she was doing was a huge risk, and it could explode in her face, but she needed to see Olivia.

Setting the cooler bag on a park bench, she stood by the edge of the huge circular garden. It bloomed with multicolored snapdragons, petunias, alyssum, miniature roses, and birds of paradise. Tables and benches were scattered all around the garden, though only a few other people had gathered here. Catherine slipped onto the bench and watched a family sitting around a table. Among them was an elderly lady in a wheelchair. She was wrapped in a pink terrycloth robe with her bald head wrapped in a matching scarf. She was pale with dark circles under her eyes. She looked weak and exhausted but couldn't stop smiling at the stories her little animated granddaughter needed to share with her.

Catherine wondered if that was what Emma would look like in a month, bald and weak. Would her sons be able to take her out in this garden? Did she even have a granddaughter to entertain her?

Catherine breathed deeply and tried to ease the tension in her chest. She opened her eyes and saw Olivia approaching along a pathway lined with bright pink peonies. Her walk was brisk and hurried, and her sunglasses shaded her eyes.

She stood over Catherine and slowly removed her sunglasses. "I got your text message. Give me three good reasons why I'm even out here talking to you."

"First reason is that it would give me the opportunity to apologize to you for being such an ass."

"That's a good start."

"Second reason is that I brought you lunch."

"I'm listening."

"The third reason would be that I couldn't stand the thought of losing you and your friendship."

"I'd hardly call what we have a friendship. It's more like an emotional tug of war." Olivia's eyes were honest but cautious. "That's not how I want things to be between us, Catherine. It completely drains me. How do you suggest we set aside preconceived notions and begin a friendship?"

"Maybe with you visiting Cocoa Cream. You could see the store I love so much. And I could pay penance with a drink of your choice."

Olivia slipped onto the bench beside Catherine. "A tall ice-cold mocha frappuccino?"

"With whipped cream."

"Now you're talking." Olivia stretched her arm along the back of the bench. "Can you tell me what makes you feel uncomfortable about me, besides my career?"

"I'd like you to let me try and understand those fears first, and when they make any sense I promise to share them with you. As I would hope you would let me know if I make you uncomfortable."

"That's fair." She paused. "How many candles did you light this morning?"

Catherine smiled. "Several. I needed all the help I could get. I didn't get much sleep last night. I'm sure you didn't fare any better."

"You're right about that. I care about you, Catherine. It's too bad that frightens you, but you're just going to have to get used to it. I want you in my life. If it's only as a friend, I guess I'll have to live with that. But please give us the time we need to understand what our friendship means before you dive into a rabbit hole without me. Can you do that for me?"

"Yes, I can."

Olivia smiled. "Good. Now, what did you bring me for lunch?"

Catherine reached into the cooler bag and pulled out a brown paper sack. "I brought you a chicken curry wrap. It's our most popular sandwich in the coffee shop. I hope you like it. I also packed a blueberry scone and a bottle of water. I figured the least I could do is make your tummy happy."

Olivia peeked inside the bag. "That sounds wonderful." She looked at her watch. "Unfortunately, I should head back."

"Thank you so much for making time in your busy day to come and talk to me. That really meant a lot to me."

"I'm glad you made it happen."

Catherine gathered her things and stood. "Let me walk you back, Dr. Carrington. Then you can let me know if there's anything else I can do to make amends."

Olivia grinned. "Now you're talking."

Thirteen

CATHERINE LOCKED HER OFFICE DOOR and said good night to the evening manager. As she headed for the bustling coffee shop, she noticed Zoë and Echo winding their way through the busy tables. The connection between them was sensuous and magnetic. The way Echo held Zoë's hand and led her through the busy room, smiling reassuringly, communicated a profound love that only they understood. Catherine smiled as they approached. "Hello, Echo and Zoë."

"Hello, Catherine," Zoë said. "This place is incredible. Is it always this crazy busy in the evening?"

"This is our usual Friday-night chaos. We love it. It's so nice to see you, now that I know your names and a little of your story." She hugged them both, then placed her hand on Zoë's tummy. "This little girl better get here soon."

"You're telling me. I feel ready to burst, and I still have two months to go."

Catherine looked from Zoë to Echo and felt them waiting. "I believe we need to talk. Do you want to sit and have a cup of coffee?"

"That would be great if you have the time," Echo said.

Catherine took their drink orders and watched them head to the only empty table.

When she returned with a tray, Echo and Zoë looked more relaxed. She handed out the drinks and slipped into the empty seat.

Echo sipped on her caramel frappuccino. "This is wonderful, thank you."

"You're very welcome."

Zoë leaned back in her chair. "This iced coffee is wonderful, too, and we've always loved your store. Now, let's dispense with the pleasantries and get down to business. What the hell's going on with you and Olivia?"

Catherine stared at each of them wide eyed. "Wow, you don't mince words." She took a breath. "What's going on with us—at least what I hope's going on with us—is that we want to be friends. It's been a roller coaster week for us, but I think we're finally on solid ground." She hesitated. "I really care for Olivia. She's bright and witty. I'm drawn to her warmth, charm, and sense of humor. I do want her as a friend."

Zoë leaned closer and touched her arm. "Will you promise us one thing?"

"Absolutely."

"Be good to her. Her last relationship ended terribly and we don't want to see her hurt again. We want to see her happy."

Echo and Zoë didn't seem ready to accept this was only a friendship. "I can't promise you that I won't hurt her. I already have. What I will promise is that I would never hurt her intentionally."

Echo set her cup down on the table. "I guess we can't ask for more than that."

"And as her friend, I'd love the opportunity to get to know the women she treasures as her sisters."

Zoë rubbed her tummy. "Well, have you eaten yet?"

"As a matter of fact I haven't, and I'm starving."

"How does Chinese food sound?"

"Sounds wonderful."

"Great then. Let's go."

Zoë and Catherine stood. Echo stayed seated. "Wait a minute. I'd like some time to browse."

Zoë cupped Echo's chin in the palm of her hand. "I'm very pregnant, very hungry, and about to get very crabby if you delay feeding me and your daughter another minute. Therefore, I highly recommend you rise from that chair and we'll make plans to come here another evening."

Echo slowly rose from her chair. "Is there any chance that my daughter is going to be just as bossy as you?"

Zoë stepped away and slung her purse over her shoulder. "Count on it."

Olivia lit the last candle on the edge of her bathtub. The soulful melody of Il Divo's song "Unbreak My Heart" filtered around her. She slipped her legs into the hot water and sat on the towel on the edge of her Jacuzzi as she typed in a text message. *Is this a good time for a friend to call?*

Olivia set the phone on the edge of the tub and slipped into the steamy bath. She let the bubbles enfold her as she leaned her head back against the tub pillow and closed her eyes. The light scent of vanilla wafted from the candles surrounding her as she completely let herself go and luxuriated in this simple pleasure.

Olivia's phone chimed for an incoming text message. She sat up, dried her hands on the towel, and checked the screen. *Absolutely.*

She smiled and entered Catherine's number.

"I understand you had an eventful evening breaking egg rolls with the crazy roommates."

"I certainly did. They're wonderful, Olivia. I can certainly understand why you love them so much."

"They really enjoyed you, too. I'm jealous I couldn't be there as well. Who the hell do they think they are going to dinner with you before I do?"

"They had more than just breaking egg rolls on their minds. They wanted to know what my intentions are with you, which surprised me a little since I'm sure you must have told them we're just friends."

"I've hardly *seen* them, Catherine. Were they really that bad?"

"They were on a mission. They grilled me for the first hour on my education, upbringing, religion, morals, beliefs, goals, and aspirations. I was just waiting for them to ask me to produce copies of my bank statements and last tax return."

Olivia closed her eyes. "Now I'm really going to kill them."

Catherine laughed. "I'm exaggerating, Olivia. They weren't nearly that bad. At least they tried not to be so overt in their quest for information. Mainly we talked about our careers and the imminent arrival of your niece. I loved hearing how they decorated the nursery with angels and teddy bears. You're blessed with true friends."

"That I am."

"Where are you right now?"

"I'm submerged in my wonderful Jacuzzi. I love my tub. It's the one place I can completely let go and relax after a busy day. You should be getting some bubbles coming through your phone any minute now."

Catherine swallowed at the thought of Olivia naked in her tub. "Tell me about your home, Olivia."

"It's quite an architectural marvel. My dads built the house in two identical wings. Each wing has four bedrooms, a sitting room, and a small kitchen. The focal point of the house is the common family room and huge kitchen, plus we have a big entertainment room, an exercise room, a library, and an indoor pool. Even with our own private wings we tend to spend whatever time we have together cocooned in the same room. I just wish I had more time to spend here."

"It sounds lovely."

Olivia was starting to recognize the aloof tone Catherine used when she became uncomfortable. "What about you, Catherine? Is your home your haven away from work?"

Catherine hesitated. "It's my oasis. It's everything I want and need."

Olivia wished she could see Catherine's eyes to try and understand what that really meant.

"Did you enjoy the Chinese food the crazy roommates brought home for you?"

"I sure did. I thoroughly enjoyed the fortune cookie they said you sent home for me."

"What did your fortune say?"

"It said beware of a beautiful Irish woman with crystal blue eyes. She'll challenge every fiber of your being."

"Liar."

"It's all in the interpretation, my Irish friend. What it really said was you're in for a wonderful surprise."

"Honestly?"

"Honestly. I'll show you the proof. What did your fortune say?"

"It said to follow my heart."

"Now isn't that interesting."

"Very. I'm putting it in the small treasure chest I keep on my desk with all my dreams and wishes. I'll show it to you when you drop by the bookstore."

"Do you care to share any of the dreams and wishes you keep in your treasure chest?"

"It's an ever changing list but the current top three are my mom's continued good health, the continued success of Cocoa Cream, and a trip to Paris. I've never been and would love to go someday."

"Your mom has certainly fulfilled her part. It sounds like Cocoa Cream is already a national treasure, so that leaves your trip to Paris. You've made the first two happen, so Paris should be a shoe-in."

"I really hope so. But if it doesn't, I'm thrilled with the first two." Catherine hesitated. "What's in the top three on your wish list?"

Olivia floated her hand through the sea of bubbles. "My current list is the safe arrival of my niece, a better balance between work and play, and last but not least a Maui vacation and an exotic island woman dressed only in a grass skirt serving me a tall icy Mai Tai."

Catherine laughed. "Your imagination knows no limits, Olivia. I like that. You must be starting to prune by now. Is the water getting chilly?"

"A bit. I haven't enjoyed a bath like this in a very long time. Thanks for joining me."

"Thanks for inviting me. Are you working this weekend?"

"I'm afraid so. It's my weekend on call. What about you?"

"I'm opening the doors of the bookstore at seven a.m."

"Well then, I should let you go. Good night, Catherine."

"Good night, Olivia," Catherine said, not wanting to hang up.

Fourteen

OLIVIA WALKED ACROSS THE PARKING LOT to the large automatic glass doors. The patio tables across the front of the store were full of patrons enjoying their specialty drinks in the balmy evening air. She stopped in the entrance-way and smiled at the plastic figurine of Friar Tuck dressed in a flowing green robe waving an Irish flag. He must have stood three feet tall and his chubby face and gregarious smile welcomed everyone.

Moving through the glass doors, Olivia felt blanketed by the smell of freshly ground coffee and the hum of excited voices. All the tables and overstuffed chairs in the coffee shop were filled with people deeply engrossed in conversation. Sarah McLaughlin's song "Fallen" filled the air with her ethereal voice and blanketed Olivia with a sense of belonging. As she worked her way through the crowd she noticed several pairs of men holding hands and a couple of women nestled in one chair together. She headed for the coffee-shop counter illuminated with a shamrock beaded light set.

"Welcome to Cocoa Cream. What can I get for you?"

"Actually, I'm looking for Catherine O'Grady. Do you know where I can find her?"

Summer pointed through the coffee shop. "That area over there inundated with lighted shamrocks is the customer-service desk. You should find her there. If not, Laura or Dana will know where she is."

"Thank you."

"Can I get you something to drink first?"

"Let me say hello to Catherine and then I promise to be back for a mocha frappuccino."

"Sounds great."

Crystal stepped in beside Summer and reached into the glass display case for a cranberry scone. She followed Summer's gaze. "Who was that gorgeous woman?"

"I don't know, but she's looking for Catherine. Why don't beautiful women like that come looking for me?"

Crystal laughed as she slipped the scone into a brown paper bag. "Because you still haven't learned to stop drooling at the sight of a gorgeous lesbian."

Summer scowled as the next customer stepped up to the counter.

Olivia made her way through the bustling coffee shop and entered the two-tier bookstore. She was in awe of it its sheer size and feeling of warmth as she admired the shamrock garland and wreaths adorning all the banisters around the store. She saw people gathered in several areas of comfortable chairs and couches arranged together in cozy sitting areas. Olivia headed for the customer-service desk and smiled at the bright green St. Patrick's Day banner draped across the front of the desk. Huge green paper shamrocks hung from the lights above the counter. A tall auburn-haired woman behind the counter hung up the telephone and turned to her. "Hello. Welcome to Cocoa Cream. How can I help you?"

"I was looking for Catherine O'Grady."

"She just stepped into our storage room. May I tell her who's looking for her?"

"Please. I'm Olivia Carrington."

The woman's eyes narrowed dangerously as she folded her arms across her abdomen. "Ah, the big mean doctor who's upset my best friend more than once."

Olivia was taken aback. She glanced at the nametag. "I believe Catherine and I have sorted things out, Laura."

"Catherine and I are very close, Dr. Carrington, and I don't enjoy seeing her upset. You best remember that. However, it did mean a lot to her that she had a chance to talk to you throughout the week. She seems to think you could be a good friend to her. You have yet to prove yourself to me."

"You obviously love her very much, Laura. I'm just beginning to get to know her but I can tell you that she's someone that I'd like to get to know better. As a friend."

Laura nodded toward the single pink rose Olivia was carrying. "Do you always give roses to your friends?"

"Not always."

They stood for a moment looking at each other.

"Okay. Why don't you browse around the store and I'll tell Catherine you're here."

"Thank you. And Laura, I really do care for her. Can you allow me that?"

Laura stepped around the counter and stood beside Olivia. "I love her, Olivia. She's been through so much with her parents and in her personal life. I want her to be happy. What she wants right now from you is friendship. Just promise me you'll listen to her, and not push her in a direction she isn't ready for."

"Promise granted."

"Okay. I'll go find her."

Laura walked through to the back of the bookstore and into the large storage room. Catherine was gingerly stretching on her tiptoes to set a stack of Patricia Cornwell paperbacks on a high shelf. She blew a strand of hair out of her eyes and tucked it behind her ear, then turned when she heard Laura walking toward her. They shared a warm smile. "Do you need me, Laura?"

"No, but it seems that Dr. Olivia Carrington would like to see you."

Catherine was startled. "She's here in Cocoa Cream?"

"Yes, she is. And she's carrying a rose. I told her to go look around the bookstore while I came to get you. That was after I gave her an earful about having to prove herself to me if she wanted to be your friend."

"Oh, Laura, you didn't."

"I sure did. I really dislike the fact that I warmed up to her by the time we were done talking. And don't you dare tell her I said that. I'd like to see her squirm when she's around me. That should keep her on her best behavior for a while."

Catherine couldn't help but laugh. "I hope you didn't totally terrify her, Laura."

"Not totally, just slightly." Laura brushed a smudge of dust off Catherine's chin. "Go clean up before you go out there and talk to that beautiful lesbian friend of yours."

Catherine brushed the dust off her hands. "Tell her I'll be out in a minute." She started for her office then stopped and turned back to Laura. "Play nice."

"Do I have to?"

Catherine shook her head and headed through the storage room door.

Fifteen

C ATHERINE FOUND HER MOTHER behind the customer-service desk.

"Have you seen Olivia, Mom?"

Dana watched the emotions wrestle with her daughter's spirit. She gently touched her cheek. "I believe she's waiting for you in the women's studies section."

Catherine walked past the mystery and science-fiction sections and turned the corner, feeling her pulse quicken as she saw Olivia nestled in an overstuffed well-worn chair, with her legs crossed at the ankles on the ottoman before her. She was dressed elegantly in a nutmeg suede blazer, sunshine yellow turtleneck, and black dress slacks. A big fluffy white traitorous cat nestled peacefully in her lap. In one hand Olivia held a copy of the *San Diego Hikers Guide;* the other gently, rhythmically stroked Maya's chin.

Catherine couldn't believe how the sight of Olivia completely strangled her ability to breathe or think. This was not how a woman should feel about a friend.

She took a deep breath and slowly approached Olivia's chair, easing herself onto the edge of the ottoman. She felt an intense heat as her hip settled against Olivia's legs. She struggled to calm her jagged nerves as Maya stretched her front paws before her and curled them rhythmically.

Olivia's face shone with a heartfelt smile. "Catherine."

"Welcome to Cocoa Cream, Dr. Carrington. Why didn't you call and tell me you were coming?"

"I was afraid you wouldn't be here. So I thought I'd just take my chances and show up. It looks like lady luck was on my side for once." She picked up the pale pink rose from the table beside her and handed it to Catherine. "This is for you."

Catherine accepted the delicate rose and brought it to her face. She closed her eyes and inhaled the beautiful fragrance. "Thank you, Olivia."

"You're very welcome. The pale pink color signifies friendship. I just wanted you to know that our conversations this week meant a lot to me."

"It's meant a lot to me, too. What do you think of our place?"

"It's incredible. It's great to see the large showing from our community here."

"We're very blessed. I was really fortunate to buy in this area of Hillcrest. The huge gay and lesbian population has embraced us and made this a popular hangout. In turn I try to have a good stock of books they might enjoy. We want them to feel like this is their home."

"You certainly have achieved that ambiance. I love all the St. Patrick's Day decorations."

"St. Patrick's Day is very special to us. It's the day we opened the bookstore. We always have a huge St. Patrick's Day celebration for our anniversary. It's actually three weeks away. If you're off that Saturday maybe you'll join us."

"I'd love to. So many people have told me about this store. I can't believe I've never been here. You really have created a very warm place." She paused and frowned slightly.

"Your cat, however, is a much better welcoming committee than your bodyguard, Laura."

"Laura told me about your conversation. I'm sorry about that. Laura's my best friend and also helps manage Cocoa Cream with my mom and me. She cares about me, Olivia. She didn't mean any harm."

"Are you kidding? I'm shocked she even let me stay to see you. When I saw your cat come toward me I thought Laura had sent her to attack. Instead she jumped into my lap and curled up into a ball."

Maya yawned hugely before tucking her paws back under her chest and looking directly at Catherine with that, "Did you need us for something?" annoyed look that only cats can pull off effortlessly. Catherine shook her head in disbelief and glared at Maya. "Traitor. I thought you were supposed to protect this store from mean people and dangerous lesbians."

Olivia laughed as she placed the open book over the arm of her chair. "How would you classify me, Ms. O'Grady? A mean person or a dangerous lesbian?"

"I wouldn't necessarily classify you as mean. Dangerous means able to do harm. Are you able to do harm, Dr. Carrington?"

Olivia luxuriated in Catherine's closeness. "I guess that depends on what you consider harm, Ms. O'Grady. Laura certainly seems capable of it."

Catherine crossed her legs and held her rose gently in her hands. "Laura's bark is worse than her bite, Olivia. Besides, she doesn't want you to know that she'd warmed up to you by the end of your conversation."

"If that's warm, I'd hate to be around her if she disliked me."

Catherine couldn't help but laugh. She glanced at the cover of Olivia's guidebook. "Do you enjoy hiking?"

"I love hiking. There are so many gorgeous trails in and around San Diego. My favorite is in Torrey Pines. But once again my big issue is finding the time. What about you? Are you a hiker?"

"I'm not a big fan of encroaching on the rough terrain that God intended for reptiles and multilegged creatures. I much prefer to pound the pavement and explore the shops intended for civilized women."

"Spoken like a true urbanite. It looks like I'll have to take you out for a walk and show you what you're missing." Olivia rubbed Maya's ear. "Do you think that's a wise idea, Maya? Or is she liable to toss me off some cliff side?"

Catherine laughed. They both looked down at Maya, sound asleep and purring like a running motor in Olivia's lap. "She never curls up like that with a stranger. She much prefers to perch on the top of a shelf or stack of books and spy on our customers. She must trust you, for some strange reason."

"Maybe she doesn't think I'm mean or dangerous."

"What does she know? She's a spoiled-rotten cat."

"Pets know, Ms. O'Grady. You could perhaps learn some things from this Persian beauty."

She pulled an envelope from her jacket pocket and handed it to Catherine. "This is for you, too."

Catherine held the card for a moment. "May I open it now?"

"Absolutely."

Catherine set the rose in her lap, slowly slipped her finger beneath the flap, and tore open the envelope. She pulled out a pale yellow sheet of stationery and carefully unfolded it. Nestled in the center of the note was a fortune. The tiny paper read, *You're in for a wonderful surprise.*

"And you doubted me," Olivia said.

Catherine smiled slowly. "I've never doubted you, Dr. Carrington. Thank you for bringing me your fortune. I'll put it in my wish chest with mine." Catherine looked down at the note.

Dear Catherine,

Thank you for helping to educate women. Knowledge is power. Power is healing. I appreciate your contribution in helping women to find the information and strength they need to battle their cancer.

Warmly,
Your friend,
Olivia

Catherine slowly refolded the note and slipped it back in the envelope with the fortune. "Thank you. That was really sweet."

"You're welcome. I meant what I wrote." Olivia watched Catherine carefully. "Have dinner with me."

"As friends?"

"Absolutely."

Catherine studied Olivia. "What if I told you I already have dinner plans?"

"What if I asked you to change them?"

"Not a hope in hell. She's having dinner with me and my family."

Olivia looked up at Laura looming above her with a stack of children's books in her arms.

Catherine laughed at the apprehensive look on Olivia's face. "Sorry, Olivia, but we do have plans. Laura has a son and daughter and I'm their godmother. I try to have dinner with them once a week. I love those two like they were my own. You wouldn't think of interfering with my plans with my godchildren, would you?"

Olivia cautiously laid her hand on her own chest. "I wouldn't think of interfering with your plans with Laura and her family."

"Glad to hear it," Laura said. "We don't welcome bossy women in our store or into our lives." She turned to Catherine. "I'll go finish tidying up the children's section. I should be done in twenty minutes."

"Sounds great. Come find me when you're ready."

"I hope you enjoy your visit, Dr. Carrington. Hopefully you'll come back again to enjoy our coffee and warm hospitality." Laura strode off with a stiff back.

"Oh, yeah, that's just one big warm fuzzy," Olivia said. "Where did you find her? The witness protection program?"

Catherine laughed. "Laura and I met in college. She's been helping us manage the store for the past four years, since her babies started school. She's very protective of me."

"No kidding." Olivia gently caressed Maya's head. "When I finally get the guts to ask a woman to dinner this is a little more animosity than I'd hoped for."

Catherine leaned forward and placed her elbows on her thighs. "Mom mentioned you'll be filling in for Ruth on Monday at the Coronado Hotel."

"Yes, unfortunately that's true. I saw that you had an announcement posted on your board for the lecture series. We appreciate that."

"You don't sound excited about the lecture."

Olivia rubbed her thumb over Maya's ear. "It's just been such a busy week. Ruth offered to fly back, but I told her that was ridiculous and that I'd do it for her."

"I loved the Coronado Hotel as a child," Catherine said. "I used to go to the beach there with my parents. I loved how many famous people had stayed at the hotel, and it even has its own ghost." She shrugged. "By the time I was a teenager I was mostly interested in the shops on Orange Avenue. I liked to imagine that Marilyn Monroe browsed through the same shops I did."

"Have dinner with me at the Coronado Hotel Monday evening after my lecture?"

Catherine inhaled sharply. "That's an expensive place to dine, Olivia."

Olivia carefully considered her approach. "But worth the dining experience."

Catherine twirled the rose in her hand before looking at Olivia. "How about a compromise? I'll meet you after your lecture and we can go for an urban-girl walk. We can stroll Orange Avenue and pick a restaurant where we'll both feel comfortable with the dining experience."

Olivia smiled. "Sounds wonderful."

"Now, shall I pay my penance and go get you something from the coffee shop?"

"That would be terrific. And I've been meaning to ask—why did you name this place Cocoa Cream?"

"When I was a kid, my mom would always make me hot chocolate, but she calls it cocoa cream. I have such fond memories of enjoying those mugs of cocoa cream in front of a roaring fire with my parents and friends. When I first dreamed of this bookstore, I dreamed of bringing people together to share those same feelings. That's how this place of gathering got its name."

"What a great story."

"Can I bring you a mug of that hot cocoa cream?"

"It's tempting, but I think I'll sample your mocha frappuccino first."

"One tall mocha frappuccino coming up. And don't expect to find a little umbrella in your drink, either."

"Damn, I was going to ask for that next, with a cherry and slice of pineapple."

"Keep fantasizing, Dr. Carrington."

Catherine walked away with a gentle sway of her slender hips that seemed to grab at Olivia's belly and heat her deep inside. *If you only knew what I'm fantasizing about, Ms. O'Grady.*

Ten minutes later Catherine returned with their drinks. "One tall ice-cold mocha frappuccino for our new customer, who Summer and Crystal did not fail to notice as she walked in."

Olivia swung her legs off the ottoman and accepted the frappuccino. "Thank you. It looks great. Who are Summer and Crystal?"

"They're my coffee-shop employees. They're too young for you, and I've never seen them in grass skirts. So, hands off my staff." Catherine seated herself on the ottoman facing Olivia. "I put an insulator sleeve around the cup so your hands won't freeze."

"That was mighty thoughtful of you, Ms. O'Grady."

They both watched Maya stretch like a slinky and saunter off Olivia's lap. She gingerly hopped onto the arm and then the back of her chair, kneading the soft, plush material several times before settling in.

Catherine shook her head. "Sorry about all the white hair on your pants. I've got a lint brush you can use before you leave."

Olivia laughed. "Not a problem."

Catherine raised her glass of ice tea. She leaned forward and tapped her drink to Olivia's. "I believe my penance has been paid."

Olivia smiled. "To good old Catholic guilt." She brought the straw to her lips and took a sip. "This is terrific, thank you."

"I can't believe you're here," Catherine said.

"Neither can I. I'm on call till seven a.m., but I wanted to see you."

"Despite what I've put you through."

"Yeah, I'm thinking I should probably get my head examined."

Catherine playfully smacked her knee.

"Although, in all fairness, Abbot, Costello, and Ruth's absence contributed to my crazy week as well."

Catherine became more serious. "It's been a life-altering week for me, Olivia. Every time we talked, I wanted to know how you were, but felt hesitant to hear about your patients. Then I thought about how my mom doesn't like to tell me about the women she works with in the Comfort Program, because she knows it makes me feel uncomfortable. I want to be a better person than that. I want to be more supportive to my mother's cause and the work you do. It may take me a while, but that's what I want to work on."

"You've been through an incredible amount of pain with both parents, Catherine. Cancer is your family history, but it doesn't have to be yours. Nobody expects you to do more than you can handle. Be kind to yourself. Give what you're capable of giving and no one will fault you for it. Especially the people who know you and love you."

"All you need is a set of pom-poms, Dr. Carrington, and you'll be set."

Olivia narrowed her eyes. "Don't make fun."

"Sorry for interrupting, ladies, but I'm about ready to go." Catherine looked up at Laura. "Okay."

"I'll go see if Dana's ready. Why don't we meet you in the coffee shop?"

"That'll be fine. I'll just be a few minutes."

"Good night, Dr. Carrington. Hopefully we'll see you here again."

"Good night, Laura. Thank you for the return invitation. I wasn't sure if you were going to blacklist me or not."

"That's yet to be determined."

Laura walked away. "I can really feel her warming up now," Olivia said.

Catherine laughed. Olivia reached for the pewter pendant resting against her chest. Catherine felt her heart beat faster at the touch. "This is lovely," Olivia said

Catherine looked down at Olivia's long slender fingers delicately balancing her pendant, tracing the cross. "It's a mustard-seed necklace. Flip it over."

Olivia gently turned the pendant around and examined the mustard seed imbedded in the enamel.

"The mustard seed is a symbol of all that can be accomplished if only you believe. My parents gave that to me on the first anniversary of our store."

"That's beautiful." Olivia brushed her thumb across the mustard seed before laying it to rest against Catherine's chest. Catherine stood hesitantly, her heart still beating hard. Olivia rose from her chair and gathered her paperback book. She bent down and stroked Maya's chin. "Thanks for the warm hospitality, Maya. Maybe you could teach Attila the Laura a thing or two."

Catherine smiled. "I'll walk you to the door, Olivia."

"That'd be great. I'll go pay for my hiking guide first."

Catherine touched Olivia's arm. "I won't hear of it. Please accept the book as a gift from me and my mom."

Olivia took a twenty-dollar bill from her wallet, folded it in half, and slipped it into Catherine's pocket. "If I don't pay for this book, Laura is liable to hunt me down. Put the change in the tip jar of the girl who made my delicious drink."

"Well, then, thank you for the tip, Dr. Carrington. I'll spend it wisely."

They walked together to the sliding glass doors.

"What time should I meet you tomorrow at the Coronado?" Catherine asked.

"My lecture should end around four-thirty. Shall we meet in the main foyer at five o'clock?"

"Sounds great."

Olivia nodded toward the café. "Your family is waiting for you."

"Good night, Dr. Carrington."

Olivia stepped through the doors and out into the cool night air, then headed across the parking lot. The traffic was steady on Fifth Avenue while groups of people walked the streets and gathered to talk. The shops lining both sides of the street were garishly lit with their doors open wide for business and the cool breeze. The sounds of the Caribbean spilled from the music store on the corner while ESPN broadcast the basketball game from the sports bar down the street.

Olivia looked back over her shoulder to the bright warmth of Cocoa Cream, washed by a wave of longing.

Sixteen

WHEN CATHERINE WAS A LITTLE GIRL, the Hotel del Coronado always made her feel like she'd walked onto the grounds of a fairy-tale castle. The massive red-peaked roofs soared upward. The pristine white building seemed to stretch forever, embraced by unending balconies. Sometimes she wished she could reclaim the pure pleasure she'd felt here as a child.

She walked along the patio, pulling her red cardigan tighter as the gentle breeze tugged at her dress. She looked beyond the expanse of white beach to the Pacific Ocean. Children played in the surf line, mindless of the cool water lapping at their toes. She leaned against the railing, letting the afternoon sun caress her face. She'd planned to arrive at the hotel only as Olivia's lecture was ending, then whisk her away to dinner on Orange Avenue, but something had drawn her here earlier.

As she watched the children on the beach, Catherine felt transported back to her childhood, when she would come here with her parents. Together they'd built magical castles with water-filled moats and towering turrets. When they were done, they'd walk along the beach and collect shells and chase the sand crabs back into their holes.

When Catherine was around thirteen, she'd begun to realize that only very wealthy people could afford to stay at the fairy-tale castle of the Hotel del Coronado. For years it had bothered her that places like this were not within her family's reach. She'd still loved to come to the beach with her parents, but she'd no longer wanted to wander around the hotel grounds.

Over time she'd come to realize how happy she was with exactly the level of wealth she'd achieved. She felt blessed with the success of Cocoa Cream, blessed that she'd been able to afford her own modest home.

The laughter of the children drew Catherine's eyes back to the beach. Her dad had loved when they buried him in the beach sand. She clearly remembered the day he'd said, "When I die, I want you two to bury me right here."

Three months after he'd died they'd chartered a boat with family and friends and headed several miles offshore. Father O'Brien prayed with everyone and blessed Aidan's ashes before Catherine and her mother tossed them to the sea. That way, her mother believed, he could always be part of the ocean and beach he loved so much.

There'd been so much turmoil and uncertainty in her life over the past several years. Things were just getting back to a sense of normalcy when a woman with beautiful amber eyes stormed into her life like a summer deluge in a tropical rainforest. Catherine deeply appreciated Olivia. She was forthright and grounded. She didn't take crap from anyone, including Catherine. She was also extremely beautiful. Catherine didn't appreciate the way her body yearned for Olivia without her permission.

She thought of Alexis, the last woman she'd trusted with her heart, the last woman she'd deeply desired. She never wanted to need or desire a woman like that again. She never wanted to be hurt again. Now she found herself staring at the waves as they washed up on the shore and faded back into the sea. If she opened her heart to Olivia, she would open herself to being hurt. But she wasn't sure she'd be able to keep Olivia just as a friend.

Catherine was jolted from her thoughts as a group of women walked across the patio and filed into the grand Hotel del Coronado. She took a deep breath and followed in behind them, stopping outside the Crown Room. Next to the door was a poster with a beautiful photo of Olivia and the caption *Dr. Olivia Carrington, Current Therapies in the Fight against Breast Cancer.* She couldn't listen to another lecture on cancer. She would just go for a walk and meet Olivia later as planned.

An older man dressed neatly in a crisp black suit closed one of the doors. "We're about to begin. Would you like to come in?"

Catherine gripped the strap of her purse. "I hadn't planned to."

He pointed to the poster. "I hear she's a great speaker. My wife died of breast cancer two years ago. I can only pray that this Dr. Olivia Carrington can give the women in there some hope."

"There's only one way to find out," Catherine said, surprising herself. She slipped into the huge flamboyant room. Chairs with gold-trimmed backs were arranged in neat rows facing the ornate, curved stage. She took a seat near the front and looked around at the noisy crowd. The room would soon be filled to capacity; Catherine guessed it could hold around two hundred people. She looked up at the carved ceilings and massive crown chandeliers. She felt torn between admiration and discomfort, remembering how, when she was a teenager, she'd felt she would never belong here.

She turned to face the stage and was soothed by the image of Thomas Kinkade's paintings changing on the huge screen like a screen saver on a computer. Within minutes the organizer of the lecture series stepped up to the microphone. She described Olivia's career and credentials. Catherine looked off to the side of the stage and saw Olivia standing in the wings, meeting her eyes with a heartwarming smile.

When the introduction ended, Olivia took her place center stage to enthusiastic applause. Catherine found herself relaxing, drawn in by Olivia's warm personality and ease with the crowd.

Olivia concluded her lecture by discussing places where people could get more information about breast cancer. She clicked from one image to the next and Catherine was stunned to see the title Cocoa Cream and all the contact information for the store.

"This place is one of my new favorite discoveries. I highly recommend that anyone who likes to visit the bookstores in the Hillcrest area stop into Cocoa Cream. It's a fabulous coffee shop and bookstore. Just ask for the owner, Catherine O'Grady, and she'll be happy to help you find what you're looking for." Catherine felt the heat rise to her face. Had Olivia planned to tell her about this, if she hadn't attended the lecture?

Olivia closed out her PowerPoint presentation and asked to have the lights turned back on. Midway through the question-and-answer session, she signaled to a woman at the back of the room.

The woman stood. "My mother-in-law has been diagnosed with lobular carcinoma in situ of her right breast," she said. "We'd like to get a second opinion but we're afraid of insulting or alienating our present doctor. We're afraid to talk to him about this and we have no clue how to go about having her seen by another specialist. Have you yourself been in this situation with your patients?"

"That's an excellent question. Yes, two of my patients over the past four years have asked for a second opinion. I would never take that as a professional insult. I see it as families wanting the best for their loved ones. I guided those two families to another specialist. Within two weeks they'd been seen and were back in my office feeling stronger and more self-assured, confident that we were on the right course of treatment. Both those women are breast-cancer survivors and I enjoy seeing them for their return visits. Now, that's my perspective on a very difficult situation. Is there anyone in the audience who has gone through that situation with a loved one and can share their personal experience?"

A heavy silence filled the room. Catherine rose and was handed a microphone by a gentleman in the aisle. She took a deep breath. "I'm Catherine O'Grady. I'm the owner of Cocoa Cream and I had no idea that Dr. Carrington was going to advertise my bookstore here today." She glared at Olivia. "Please don't visit the store all at once. We'll run out of coffee cups." The crowd laughed and Catherine turned to face the woman at the back.

"My mother was diagnosed with infiltrating ductal carcinoma of the right breast five years ago by a colleague of Dr. Carrington's, Dr. Ruth Ratcliff. We were in shock but we wanted a second opinion before we went ahead with any treatment. We talked to Dr. Ratcliff and decided to take my mother to the Hailey Center in Phoenix. It's an exceptional cancer center. The doctors there were fabulous with us. They reviewed my mother's mammograms and concurred with Dr. Ratcliff's diagnosis and plan of care. We needed that reassurance. It definitely empowered us and made us feel even more confident with Dr. Ratcliff. In the bookstore, I have all the contact information for the Hailey Center and other doctors who could give your mother-in-law a second opinion. Before we leave tonight, I'll give you my business card so you can contact me at your leisure."

Tears filled the eyes of the woman at the back of the room as she whispered, "Thank you."

Olivia answered several more questions and thanked everyone for attending. The audience rose and applauded.

Catherine remained standing as the crowd began to file out. A number of women surrounded Olivia on the stage. Catherine reached for her purse beneath her chair and headed for the woman at the back of the room.

Seventeen

OLIVIA SEARCHED THE MAIN FOYER and saw Catherine standing alone on the deck facing the ocean. Her long knit red dress hugged her feminine contours to perfection and sent a rush of heat cascading through Olivia's chest and belly. No woman had ever affected her on sight the way Catherine did. She filled Olivia with a warmth and need that came from deep within. She was so dynamic and multifaceted. She was challenging, frustrating, and exhilarating. Olivia wanted this woman, but she knew she needed to move slowly. And she knew by the way she was standing that Catherine was humming with barely suppressed anger.

Olivia approached and stood close behind her. "Thank you for coming to the lecture, Catherine. I was really surprised to see you in the audience."

Catherine continued to stare out at the sailboats dancing with the wind. "And I was really surprised to see Cocoa Cream as part of your presentation. You're just bent and determined to test me, aren't you?"

"If that was your idea of a test, you passed with flying colors."

Catherine slowly turned to face her. "I would've liked a little forewarning, Olivia."

"If you think for one second that I was going to interrupt your dinner with Laura and her family last night to ask your permission to talk about Cocoa Cream, you're nuts. I'd like to live a long and healthy life." Olivia touched a strand of Catherine's hair resting on her shoulder. "Thank you for helping that woman in the audience."

"I understood what she was going through. It felt right to help her."

"Do we still have a dinner date—as friends, of course?"

Catherine didn't answer. Instead, she turned and stared out at the multicolored sails propelling the boats along the choppy waters. She didn't know what she wanted. She wanted to stay mad, and she wanted to keep her heart open. She wanted to be home, curled on her own comfortable couch, and she wanted to be here with Olivia. She took a deep breath. "Sure. Where would you like to eat?"

"Your choice, since you're so averse to a nice meal at the Coronado."

"Do you like Mexican?"

"Absolutely. Any place in mind?"

"Do you know Miguel's? It's in the courtyard of the old El Cordova Hotel."

"No, but I've heard about it. Lead the way."

Catherine felt herself relaxing as they headed south on Orange Avenue with the rest of the crowd, peeking in boutique windows and browsing the specialty shops. She found herself thinking that she and Olivia could in fact be friends, but only if they stayed away from hospitals and lecture halls.

They found the cobblestone path to Miguel's and were quickly seated in the bustling colorful courtyard. A waiter placed a basket of chips and a dish of traditional salsa and white cheese dip on their table.

Olivia looked around. "This place is amazing."

Catherine turned Olivia's menu over for her. "Look at the list of specialty drinks."

Olivia scanned the list. "'Millionaire' and 'billionaire' margaritas? I'm surprised you even let us come here. I would think that could just about tip you over the edge."

"Lucky for you they're reasonably priced and delicious. I think we should show some restraint and have the millionaire."

Olivia laughed. Catherine dipped a nacho chip into the thick cheese dip and bit into it with pleasure. "I know it's not the Coronado, but believe me, the food here is wonderful."

"Actually, I hate the Coronado."

Catherine was startled. "What?"

Olivia shrugged. "I used to love it, but the last time I lectured at the Coronado was one of the worst days of my life. Are you up to hearing a long, sad story?"

"Of course.

"It was two years ago. Jessica and I had been together for four years. She works in cancer research. We met when we were both involved in a project for Memorial-Sloan Kettering in New York. Jessica was an only child. She'd met my family and when I talked to her about moving back to San Diego and living in one house with Zoë and Echo she was excited. She was involved in the plans of the new house and we all moved in four years ago."

Olivia stared down at her cutlery. "It didn't take long for me to realize it was all too much for Jessica. She'd had me to herself for four years and she wasn't very happy about sharing me with my family. She began to resent the time we spent with my dads. She began to get very jealous of my close relationships with Zoë and Echo. I offered to move out and get us a house of our own. She didn't seem too excited by that, either.

"Two years ago, when I'd committed to the lecture series, I booked us a room at the Coronado. I thought we could spend the weekend together and try to work things out between us. Jessica was supposed to meet me there. I was unpacking before my lecture in a beautiful suite, feeling hopeful. Then I found the letter she'd put in my suitcase, telling me she was very unhappy and was moving on."

The waiter returned with glasses of water. Catherine placed her hand on her menu. "We would both like a millionaire margarita. We'll just need a few more minutes to look at the menu."

"Certainly."

Catherine turned to Olivia. "Then what happened?"

Olivia stared off through the courtyard. "I tried to call her on her cell but she never answered. When I called home, Echo told me that she must have moved out during the day because all her things were gone."

Catherine reached for Olivia's hand. "I'm sorry, Olivia."

"Me, too. It was hard. I felt like I failed her. I spent a lot of time wondering what I did wrong and what I could have done better. I wondered if I should have put more into our relationship or if it just wasn't meant to be."

"What did you do about your lecture?"

"What could I do? I sat in the suite and felt numb. I wanted to get the lecture over with and go home, but I had no desire to go home and find Jessica gone. That's why I hate the Coronado."

"Were you ever able to get in touch with Jessica?"

"She called me a week later to let me know she'd moved back to New York. She asked me to forgive her for leaving the way she did. I don't believe in hanging on to someone who doesn't want to be there. I wished her well and we've never talked again." She took a breath. "It was so good to see you in the audience tonight, Catherine. It made things so much easier."

"I'm glad. I had no intention of being in that audience, Olivia. I came early, and you could say I was guided. Now that I've heard the whole story, I feel guilty for acting so cold when your lecture was over."

"I like the way your Catholic guilt keeps you in check."

"Don't make light of my faith."

"I'm not making light of it. Honestly. I admire your faith. It seems very much a part of who you are."

Catherine studied Olivia. "What about you, Olivia? Do you consider yourself religious?"

"It depends on what you mean by religious. Spiritual, maybe. But no, I'm not drawn to religion. It's simply not the way I'm put together, and I don't think it's just my training in science and medicine. Is that hard for you to take in?"

"A little. I've always found so much solace in the church."

"It doesn't distress you that so many religious people would judge you for your lifestyle?"

"I know without a doubt that God doesn't judge me. That's all that matters."

Olivia looked thoughtful. "Maybe my resistance to religion dates back to childhood. My mom took me regularly to church when I was a kid. When I was sixteen, she had an affair with her boss. I was furious that she could pray in church one day, and betray my dad the next. "

"You hinted at a rift with your mom that day in the chapel," Catherine said. "I've wanted to ask about it."

"It was awful. She decided to start a new life with her boss. They up and moved to Las Vegas within a couple of weeks and sent me and my dad into a tailspin. I'll never understand how it could be so easy for her to walk away from both of us."

Olivia felt sixteen again, swallowed by teenage anger and the hurt of desertion. "It took me a long time to realize I needed to forgive her so I could shed my resentment and anger. Then I started to appreciate how close it brought my dad and me together."

Olivia had told this story only to her closest friends. It felt so easy and right to tell it to Catherine.

"I'm glad you could find a silver lining."

The waiter returned. Catherine ordered the shrimp fajitas and Olivia ordered the carne asada. They spoke of lighter matters as they ate, laughing together.

At the end of the meal, the waiter placed a dish of flan with two spoons between them. "I'll be right back with the bill, señoritas."

"Thank you," Olivia said. She picked up both spoons and handed one to Catherine.

Catherine dug her spoon into the creamy dessert. She tasted the first spoonful and closed her eyes. "You won't believe how good this is." She slowly opened her eyes to find Olivia watching her. Impulsively, she dug her spoon in again and held it before Olivia's mouth. Olivia parted her lips and took the flan. Catherine stared at those full sensuous lips then forced herself to lean back in her chair and look away.

Olivia felt Catherine's unease and wanted to fuel the tension sizzling between them. She was dying to know what it would feel like to take this woman in her arms and devour her rather than the tasty flan between them. She scooped her spoon into the dessert and raised it. Catherine's gaze came back to Olivia's face. She hesitated a moment, then opened her alluring mouth. Olivia thought she was going to explode with her desire for this woman. She let her hand drop to the table as the waiter arrived and placed the bill between them. She and Catherine both reached for the plastic tray, their fingers brushing.

Olivia slid the bill away from Catherine. "I believe this is my treat. I was the one who asked you to dinner."

"Thank you, then." She smiled. "I hope you have enough money to cover the millionaire margaritas. Speaking of money." Catherine pulled a slip of paper from her purse and slid it in front of Olivia.

Olivia picked up the paper and scanned the information. "Why do I have a receipt from St. Joseph's Church in the amount of twenty dollars in my name?"

"My mom went there today. I asked her to donate your twenty dollars to the church. Think of how many candles Father O'Brien can buy with that money."

Olivia laughed. "You gave my twenty dollars to the church instead of using it to pay for my new book?"

"I certainly did. I even included the tip you offered me for making your drink."

"Man, I have to watch what you do with my money in the future."

Olivia's cell phone chimed. She quickly pulled it out of its leather case and looked at the display. "It's the girls. They left a text message that it's important."

Catherine frowned. "You better call them right away."

Olivia hit the preset number for home and held the phone to her ear. "Zoë, what's up?"

"I'm sorry for interrupting your dinner, Olivia. But we have quite a dilemma here at the house and you're not going to be happy."

"What dilemma? Are you guys okay?"

"We're fine, but Abbott and Costello are not. The workmen brought the new vanity into our bathroom and began installing it today. Somehow Abbott and Costello have managed to wedge themselves into the base and we can't get them out."

Olivia dropped her face into her hand and groaned. "You've got to be kidding me, Zoë. Ruth's flying home tonight, and you're telling me her beloved rodents are stuck in the vanity? How the hell did Abbott and Costello get into your bathroom in the first place?"

Catherine hid her laughter behind her hands.

"Now's probably not a good time to start pointing fingers, Olivia. We've all been here with Brady and Austin for the past hour and a half trying to get those two damn creatures out of this mess."

"Why can't you just move the vanity away from the wall and go after them?"

"The vanity is eight feet long and the workmen permanently fixed it to the wall, Olivia. Why do you think we called Brady and Austin? We thought we could get them to dismantle at least a part of it so we can go after the ferrets. But there's no way. The opening in the bottom of the vanity is about four inches from the floor. The trim along the bottom of the vanity hasn't been put on and that's how Abbott and Costello got into the woodwork."

Olivia leaned her elbows on the table and pressed the phone against her forehead.

Catherine reached for the cell phone. "Hello, Zoë. This is Catherine."

"Hello, Catherine. I'm really sorry for interrupting your dinner. We just thought you guys should know and see if you can come up with any bright ideas. We've just about exhausted our vast resources here."

"Have you tried bringing their food nearby so they can smell it?"

"Echo reached in as far as she could and put their food inside. They won't bite. They're having too much of a good time watching us sweat here."

"Can you actually see where they're lodged?"

"Echo shined a light under the vanity and saw where they've happily taken up camp."

"I think I have an idea. Hang on one second. Olivia, how long will it take us to get to Cocoa Cream from here and then to your house?"

"About forty-five minutes."

"Zoë, tell everyone to hang on tight. Olivia and I'll be there within the hour."

"Okay, Catherine, we look forward to seeing you soon."

Catherine handed Olivia her phone. "I think I have a plan."

Eighteen

OLIVIA CHECKED HER REARVIEW MIRROR to make sure Catherine was right behind her before she guided her black Escalade through the wrought-iron security gates. Olivia drove beneath the arched tower entranceway and parked by the front flagstone steps. She watched Catherine park behind her. Olivia opened the driver door to Catherine's mint green Volkswagen bug. She extended her hand. "Welcome to twenty-five Carriage House Lane."

Catherine stepped from her car, taking in the sprawling estate of flagstone walls and Spanish tiled roofs, not knowing what to think. "Wow. I'm starting to understand why you call your home a monstrosity."

In fact, the place was beautiful. The huge windows and turret towers added a medieval air. The massive double front door was embossed with rainbow-colored beveled glass that gleamed like crystals. But she was taken aback by the home's sheer size. Her house could probably fit in the four-car garage. "Your home looks like a Spanish palace fit for royalty."

"No royalty, just a bunch of crazy lesbians live here. Come on, let me show you inside." Olivia grabbed Maya's pet carrier from the back seat of Catherine's car and guided her up the front steps.

Olivia opened the front door and followed Catherine inside. She set Maya's pet carrier down on the tiled floor and closed the door behind them. Catherine stared up at the stained-glass dome adorning the ceiling of the entranceway.

"What do you think?" Olivia asked.

"This must be amazing when the sun shines through all that stained glass."

"It's about time you both got here," Echo said.

Catherine looked through the spacious living room to see Zoë and Echo approaching. Their presence made the house seem much less daunting.

They all hugged. "Hello, ladies. It's so nice to see you both again," Catherine said. She placed her hand on Zoë's rounded belly. "Hello, little one."

Zoë slid Catherine's hand around her belly to the spot where she could feel the baby moving.

Catherine smiled as she felt something bumping against the palm of her hand. "How are you feeling?"

"I feel like the Pillsbury Dough girl. Another eight weeks seems like an eternity right now."

Echo cautiously slipped her arm around Olivia. "Are you angry?"

"I'm pissed, and I'm holding you both directly responsible for the rescue and capture of two menacing pains in the butt."

"Don't worry about Olivia," Catherine said. "Maya's here to save the day." She pointed down at Maya patiently waiting to be freed from her prison.

Zoë laughed. "What a great idea."

Catherine knelt down and opened the cage door, then reached in for Maya. The beautiful Persian settled happily into her mistress's arms.

"Please tell me that cat is going to be the answer to our prayers."

Catherine turned toward the wide-open spacious kitchen and saw two very handsome men walk toward them. Both stood taller than Olivia, and Catherine knew right away which one was Olivia's biological father by his smiling amber eyes.

Austin was slightly taller, with short, thick, light brown hair and vibrant blue eyes. Catherine could sense the loving energy between them as they walked close together.

"Catherine O'Grady, I'd like you to meet my dads, Brady and Austin."

Catherine cradled Maya against her shoulder and extended her free hand to Brady. "It's a pleasure to meet you, sir. I can see where Olivia gets her beautiful eyes."

"It's a pleasure to finally meet the girl Olivia's been talking about."

She wasn't sure she was ready for Olivia to be talking about her to her fathers, but she composed herself and turned to Austin. "And you, sir, gave Olivia her beautiful smile."

Austin beamed. "Why thank you, Catherine. I've always believed Olivia looks more like me."

"Can we please dispense with the pleasantries and see if Catherine's plan will work?" Echo asked.

The entire entourage made its way up the spiral staircase. Two hallways stretched away from the landing. Catherine glanced with curiosity through half-open doors as they followed the hallway to the right, then entered Echo and Zoë's master suite. She absorbed the warmth in the modern design and decided it suited them both.

They stepped into the bathroom and walked carefully across the sheets of plastic covering the floor. Catherine stopped before the steps leading to the huge marble Jacuzzi. Behind it, three panels of stained glass formed exquisite sunburst patterns. Two people could just fit in her own bathroom at one time. Here, six people and a cat were milling around trying to figure out the fate of two wayward ferrets.

"Everything's really starting to come together, ladies," Olivia said.

Echo grinned widely. "Can you imagine how much fun we'll have in here? Hours and hours of pure sensual pleasure. And now with a longer vanity I can plunder Zoë right up against the mirror."

Catherine couldn't help but laugh. "Zoë, you lucky girl, you."

Zoë rubbed her tummy. "She'll be lucky to even get me up on that vanity, in this condition."

Olivia stared at them. "Will you guys please behave yourselves in front of our company?"

Echo grabbed the flashlight. "Please, Catherine's hardly company. Come see the unwanted bathroom guests."

Olivia removed her jacket and hung it on the rack behind the door. She got down to her knees and lay beside Echo on her belly. They both peered under the cabinet. "I see them. They look terrified."

Echo got to her knees and helped Olivia up. "If they're so terrified then why don't they get the hell out?"

Catherine looked down into the hole in the cabinet where the sinks were to be installed. "Echo, did you take the food out from under the vanity?"

"I did."

Austin stood beside Catherine. "I hope Maya's a good hunter."

"She's the best. We once found a mouse in the storage room of the bookstore. She chased that thing for hours till it finally took off out the back door and never came back."

Brady rubbed Maya's chin. "You're a regular Xena the Warrior Princess. How do you want to handle this, Catherine?"

"I think we should all stand away from the vanity. Echo, if you'll flash the light under there again I'll let Maya get sight of them. Then I'll grab her and put her by the hole where the sink belongs and see if she can scare those two out. Do Abbott and Costello have their own pet carrier?"

Echo headed for the door. "I'll go get it."

Catherine looked at everyone standing by the Jacuzzi tub. "That way we can hopefully grab them as they run out and put them in a safe place."

Echo returned with the pet carrier, closing the door firmly behind her. "Got it."

"Good. Place it over by the tub, Echo. Brady and Austin, is there something we can put under the vanity to block that opening so they can't get back under?"

Austin found a long piece of wood by the shower stall. "This is the trim they plan on installing tomorrow. Brady and I'll wedge it in front once those two find their way to freedom."

"Sounds like a plan. Okay, if everyone's ready this might be a good time for a quick prayer."

Olivia scratched her head. "Wait, this plan makes me nervous. What if something happens to any of the animals?"

Echo leaned back against the vanity. "Do you have a better idea?"

Olivia frowned. "No."

"Have faith," Catherine said.

Olivia sighed. "If this plan works, I swear I'll donate enough money to St. Joseph's Church for Father O'Brien to buy a hundred candles."

Everyone looked at Olivia in bewilderment as Catherine laughed. "You're on, Dr. Carrington."

"Okay, Echo. Lights, action, camera."

Echo shone the light beneath the cabinet. Catherine lowered Maya down beside her. The well-orchestrated plan then took on a life of its own. The screech that came from Abbott and Costello was enough to wake the dead. Maya flattened her body as much as she could and tried valiantly to wedge herself under the cabinet. Catherine grabbed her, pulled her back, and barely managed to place the writhing cat in the empty frame for the sink. Maya took off through the opening and into one of the cabinets, scratching like a creature hellbent on digging to China to get to those ferrets through the thin paneling of wood.

Echo was once again flashing the light when both Abbott and Costello tore out from under the vanity and ran right across her head. Echo screamed as the slinky moving fur balls headed for the exit. They couldn't stop fast enough and slid head first into the closed door, then rolled across the bathroom floor like a pair of furry barrels before scrambling onto their feet. Echo screamed, "Grab them!"

Maya poked her head out through the opening and dove off the vanity in hot pursuit. Catherine tried to grab her and just missed.

Abbott dove behind the toilet bowl. Olivia dropped to her knees, reached around, and grabbed him by the scruff of his neck. She tried pulling him out and banged her head against the toilet bowl just as Maya lurched off the toilet seat, bounced off Olivia's back, and darted for Abbott. Olivia fell backward, hit her head against the wall, and tucked Abbott under her arm to protect him from Maya. Catherine grabbed Maya, hauled her away from Abbott, and shoved her into her pet carrier.

Squeals and laughter erupted from the other side of the room. Catherine spun to see Costello slinking at warp speed around the edge of the Jacuzzi. Echo jumped in after him, sliding around as she tried to corner the elusive ferret. She lunged for him. He leapfrogged off the tub, dove onto the vanity, and attempted to escape back into the opening just as Brady nabbed him by the scruff of his neck. Brady carried him to the ferret's pet carrier and shoved him inside.

Austin grabbed Abbott from Olivia and tossed him in with his accomplice. They secured the door. Applause and laughter vibrated off the ceramic tile walls.

Olivia was holding her head in her hands. Catherine knelt before her. "Are you okay, Olivia?"

"Just ducky, thank you for asking. Welcome to my life and my family."

Catherine laughed and helped Olivia to her feet, realizing that she did feel welcome to this family.

Olivia brushed off her pants. "I swear to God, if anyone tells Ruth what happened in here tonight, I'll kill you."

Echo picked up the ferrets' pet carrier. "There wouldn't be anything left of us if we did tell Ruth. Come on, everyone, let's get out of this construction zone."

She and Zoë and the dads filed out the door. Olivia brushed a smudge of dirt from Catherine's cheek. "Let's go into my bathroom and clean up. We're both covered in plaster dust."

Catherine swallowed and nodded.

Nineteen

CATHERINE AND OLIVIA PAUSED at the top of the spiral staircase. Catherine rested her forearms on the glossy banister, looking down into the huge family room.

Olivia set down Maya's pet carrier and stepped next to Catherine, resisting the urge to touch her. "I sense this may be one of those things that makes you uncomfortable, Catherine. Never in my wildest dreams did I imagine living in a place this huge. But when I come home to this house, to Echo and Zoë, to the reflection of the love of my dads, all the stress of my day goes away. Can you understand that?"

Catherine nodded. "I think I'm beginning to."

Olivia took Catherine's hand. "Come on. I'll show you my place. But please remember I didn't expect to have a visitor."

They toured the three spare bedrooms, kitchen, and sitting room before stepping into the master bedroom at the end of the hall.

Catherine felt both cautious and excited as she entered Olivia's private world. Framed pictures decorated one wall— Olivia's dads in tuxedos gazing at each other as if sharing a private moment; Zoë, Echo, and Olivia with arms entwined on a tropical beach; and a younger Olivia with possibly her grandmother sitting close together on an old porch swing.

Catherine ran her fingers along the footboard of Olivia's king-size four-poster mahogany bed. On one half of the bed, the floral print duvet and sheets were in total disarray. A pink tank top and pink-and-white-striped boxers sat heaped near the pillow. A half-empty bottle of water sat on the bedside table and a pair of sheepskin slippers were piled on the floor. A huge print of a pathway weaving through a forest adorned the wall at the head of the bed.

She felt the nervous tension envelop her as she walked to the fireplace framed in white-and-black swirled marble. On either side of the fireplace, thin panes of glass showcased the lush back yard. She envisioned Olivia's nights in this magnificent room and felt a heated excitement tingle her skin.

"Sorry about the mess," Olivia said.

"Don't apologize. Your room says so much about you."

"What—that my life is in chaos?"

Catherine laughed. "No. That you lead a busy life."

"You're being kind." Olivia gestured behind them. "The bathroom's this way."

Catherine followed Olivia into a spacious bathroom that mirrored the design of Zoë and Echo's. She joined her at the double sinks at the long vanity of swirled cream marble. They washed their hands at the same time. Olivia grabbed two plush forest green hand towels and handed one to Catherine. "I'm going to slip out of this suit into something more comfortable. Sorry about the plaster dust on your beautiful dress."

Catherine looked down. "Don't worry, it's washable."

"I'll be right back. Make yourself at home."

Catherine placed her towel back on the rack beside Olivia's. She touched the edge of a Post-it note stuck to the mirror and read. *"As one person I cannot change the world, but*

I can change the world of one person." Paul Shane Spear. How fitting, she thought.

She walked to the edge of the huge Jacuzzi. A bottle of bubble bath and shower gel were on the rim of the tub bedside a bar of Dove soap. In a far corner sat several candles and an iPod perched in a speaker. She envisioned Olivia immersed in bubbles the day she'd called. She unscrewed the bottle of pearberry shower gel and inhaled. This was the pleasant scent she had smelled on Olivia before.

Adjacent to the Jacuzzi was an expansive glassed-in shower. On a shelf inside were bottles of shampoo, conditioner, face scrub, a razor, and a back brush.

Catherine ran her fingers along a white terrycloth robe hanging outside the shower. She turned and saw Olivia standing in the doorway, dressed in a pair of form-fitting Levi's and black short-sleeved blouse.

Olivia smiled. "So now you've seen where I live. Except that I still have to show you around downstairs. You aren't too overwhelmed, are you?"

Catherine wasn't overwhelmed at all. She loved how full this house was of warmth and life. A true, loving family lived within its walls. "I expected to be, but I'm not. It's a beautiful home."

"I'm glad. I hadn't planned to show you this house so soon, Catherine. And I never in a million years thought the first time you met my dads we'd all be sprawled on a bathroom floor chasing two damn ferrets. Not to mention bouncing my head off the toilet bowl and the wall."

Catherine tentatively touched Olivia's temple. "Is your head okay?"

"It's fine. But I felt like a pinball for a while there."

Catherine couldn't help but laugh. "We should have filmed that whole fiasco. We'll be laughing about this for years."

Olivia looked seriously into Catherine's eyes. "I hope so."

Catherine looked away, her heart beating hard.

"How would you like a cup of coffee or tea?" Olivia said lightly. "We both could probably use one after that fiasco."

"I'd love a cup of tea."

They descended the spiral staircase to the foyer, where Austin and Brady were getting ready to leave.

"We've had way too much fun tonight, girls," Brady said. "We're heading home."

He took Catherine into his arms and hugged her close. "Good night, Catherine. It was such a pleasure meeting you. I'm thrilled your plan worked."

"I am, too." She turned to Austin. "Good night, Austin. I hope to see you both again soon. In fact, we're having a big celebration on St. Patrick's Day in the bookstore. It's our tenth anniversary and I'd love for you both to share in the festivities with us."

"Invitation accepted with pleasure," Austin said.

They both waved as they headed out the door.

Echo poked her head around the corner. "Ladies, tea's being served in the living room."

The four of them settled into the semicircular camel couches, Catherine and Olivia across from Echo and Zoë.

Zoë poured them each a cup of tea, then raised her glass of milk. "To our successful rescue mission and to new friends." They clinked cups and sipped to their success.

Catherine set her cup of tea down on the coffee table. "Have you ladies decided on a name for your daughter yet?"

Zoë beamed at Echo. "Yes, we have. We're going to name her Chloe."

"That's such a beautiful name."

Echo gathered Zoë in close. "We think so, too."

"Please tell me if this question is too personal, but I've always dreamed of having my own children and I'm fascinated to know how lesbians decide where they'll get the sperm."

Echo leaned her head against Zoë's. "It was a pretty simple decision for us. My chief of staff has always been my greatest mentor and someone Zoë and I consider a dear friend. He's sixty and has been married to his high-school sweetheart for forty years. They have six children who are all grown and have their own families. When I first told him that Zoë and I were thinking about having children and were going to research sperm banks, he just thought that was absurd. He offered us his sperm and said he would be happy to sign over his parental rights to us. His wife totally supported that plan. So when Zoë and I were ready almost seven months ago, I handed him a pink baby shower gift bag with a specimen cup and the current issue of Playboy. I told him when he was up to it we would be forever grateful to him and his wife for the gift he was about to give us."

Catherine laughed. "That's an amazing story."

Zoë sipped on her milk. "He's an amazing man. He's extremely intelligent and in excellent health so we knew he would be a great donor. His sperm are obviously just as spry, because I got pregnant the first try."

Echo gave her a shocked look. "I believe I deserve some credit for the success of that union."

Zoë leaned her head against Echo's face. "You were amazingly skillful with that turkey baster."

Echo beamed with pride. "Thank you very much."

Olivia rolled her eyes. "That definitely falls into the too-much-information category."

Catherine turned to Olivia. "What about you, Olivia? Have you ever thought about having children?"

Olivia hesitated for a moment. "I haven't. For whatever reason, it's not something I've dreamed about. I love children, but I know myself, I know the challenges on my time. I think my role in life is to be an aunt."

Catherine nodded, not sure what to say, not sure how she felt.

Zoë tried to cover her yawn. "Is it bedtime yet, baby?"

Echo kissed her forehead. "It sure is, sweetheart." She rose to her feet and extended her hand to Zoë. "We're going to say good night, ladies. It's been a pleasure, but we're beat."

"We hope to see you soon, Catherine," Zoë said.

"I'd like that very much."

Zoë slipped her hand into Echo's as they headed up the spiral staircase.

Twenty

"YOU HAVE AN INCREDIBLE FAMILY," Catherine said. "I happen to think so as well."

Catherine swallowed hard. "You must be tired, Olivia. I should probably get going before it gets much later."

"I'm never tired when I'm with you. Stay with me a little longer."

They settled back onto the couch. Catherine tucked her legs under her and wrapped her hands around her warm cup of tea.

"I told you about Jessica," Olivia said. "What about you? When was your last relationship?"

Catherine hesitated a moment, thinking back to that difficult time. "It started eight years ago, and ended two years ago. When my father was in his final stages of cancer, we wanted to get him home to be with us. The nurses arranged for us to meet with a social worker to make those plans."

Catherine was surprised at how important it felt to share her story with Olivia. She needed her to understand why she was so cautious with relationships. "Her name was Alexis. She was incredible. She helped us get my dad home in a matter of days. Shortly after he died she called to check up on us. We met for dinner. Then we started spending a lot of time together.

"Alexis has a daughter named Kayla. She'll be ten this year. I adored them both. A year after we met we moved into a rental house together and started our life as a family.

"We'd been together for two years when my mother was diagnosed. In the beginning Alexis was really supportive. Then she started resenting all the time I spent away from her and Kayla. I thought she understood that my mom needed me. Apparently I was wrong."

Olivia was listening quietly and attentively, which gave Catherine the courage to continue. "Even after Dana finished her treatments and was doing better, Alexis was still distant. My relationship with Kayla grew stronger and Alexis and I grew further apart. I figured it would just take time and we would eventually get back what we lost. I don't think she understood how scared I still was, how much I needed her support. She never talked to me about any of it. Communication is so important between women, and Alexis and I had a major meltdown in that area."

Catherine took a breath. Now that she'd started her story, she needed to tell Olivia the whole thing. "One morning Alexis forgot her cell phone at home. I was driving it over to her office for her when it rang. The name on the display was Barbara. I answered the call, which obviously shocked Barbara, who gave me the lame excuse of a wrong number. I scrolled through the call log and it became quite apparent that Barbara had called Alexis many times. The nature of their relationship was clear through the few text messages I read. When I handed Alexis her phone I told her she should probably call Barbara back, that by now she might even be over her shock at me answering. That night, Alexis admitted that she'd been having an affair with Barbara while I'd been busy with my mom.

"I was a wreck. I felt so betrayed. One week later I moved out, and I understand that Barbara moved in."

Olivia shook her head, her expression both fierce and compassionate. "I can only begin to imagine how difficult that was for you."

"I thought I was going to lose my mind. But I quickly saw the people in my life who truly cared about me. My mom was my greatest source of strength. Laura and everyone at the store were wonderful. I wouldn't have made it through without their love and kindness."

"I hope that Alexis knows what she's lost."

Catherine shrugged. "I haven't talked to her since. But I do miss Kayla. The hardest part of that breakup was saying good-bye to her and not being able to explain why her mother was doing this to us. I fear she feels I abandoned her. That's the part that tears my heart out."

"I'm so sorry, Catherine."

"Me too. The only good thing that came out of that mess was that it motivated me to buy my own house. It was a financial stretch, but I knew I needed to take the plunge. I'd talked to Alexis about us buying a home together and she kept putting me off. Then my mom got diagnosed and everything got put on hold. It's a modest little house just a few blocks from my mom's, but it's home. It was a place of healing for me and now it's my haven from this crazy world."

"I look forward to seeing it."

"I look forward to showing it to you."

Catherine touched the gold links on Olivia's watch. "What's the most important thing you learned from your relationship with Jessica?"

Olivia thought for a moment. "I learned to make sure the next woman I share my life with is a better fit. Which doesn't mean I think we should have identical passions and lifestyles. Partners need to complement, not always compromise like Jessica and I did. I need peace in my next relationship, not constant conflict. It completely drained me. I want to pour my energy and love into a relationship, not drain it with resentment and regrets."

"We both learned some valuable lessons," Catherine said.

The large oak ornate mantel clock chimed softly twelve times. "I should probably get going home. We both have to work in the morning."

"What if I asked you to stay?"

Catherine felt a rush of desire for Olivia, but shook her head. "I'm not ready for that, Olivia. My heart isn't ready. I don't know that I'm ready to trust and commit again. I really care about you. Since we first met, I've wanted to run from you yet you kept drawing me in. Your warmth and kindness embrace me. Your personality and sense of humor charm me. But what I need now from you more than anything is your friendship. I want to spend time strengthening that with you."

"And if I told you my heart is ready for more?"

"I'd feel overwhelmed. Please be patient and accept that I need to face my fears at my own pace."

Olivia leaned forward and skimmed the soft pad of her thumb across Catherine's chin. "I would love to take the time to explore our friendship. But let me tell you right now, I want you. I'm not a very patient person when I crave something, Ms O'Grady. Be forewarned. But I'll try to respect your wish for time."

"Thank you."

Catherine eased herself off the couch and extended her hand to Olivia. They walked hand and hand to the front foyer. Olivia retrieved Catherine's red cardigan and held it as she slipped into the sleeves.

Catherine straightened her cuffs and fidgeted with the buttons at her waist. She looked up at Olivia and was overcome by her need for this woman. She was never going to hold fast to her plea for time if she stood in this aura of yearning. She felt all logic slip from its tenuous hold. She inhaled deeply as she took a step back. "Good night, Olivia. Thank you for a wonderful evening, ferrets and all."

Olivia tilted her head. "Good night, Catherine. I enjoyed you immensely this evening."

Catherine quickly grabbed Maya's carrier, headed for the door, and unlocked the bolt. She jerked the door open and stood with her back to Olivia. She wanted to run, but her body refused to cooperate. She sensed Olivia behind her even before she felt her press her body against her back, closing the door quietly with their motion, easing the carrier from her fingers and onto the floor.

Olivia put her hands on the door on either side of Catherine's shoulders. She brushed her lips against her ear and then her neck. Catherine leaned back into her, a surge of searing heat dancing across her skin. Each touch of Olivia's moist lips sent trembles through her body.

Olivia turned Catherine in her arms and pressed her back against the door. "Kiss me."

Catherine was defenseless. She took Olivia's face in her hands. She skimmed her thumbs beneath those torrid amber eyes, and along the outline of her jaw. She felt the heat of Olivia's hands as they formed to her hips and glided across her lower back, pulling her away from the door. She leaned into Olivia's embrace, unable to resist their shared desire.

Catherine touched her lips to Olivia's and plunged into a kiss that rendered her mindless. The softness of Olivia's lips, the gentleness of her touch, the unmitigated desire churned deep in Catherine's soul.

They both struggled to catch their breath as Olivia pulled Catherine in tight and held her with her waning strength. She brushed her lips against Catherine's temple. "That certainly did nothing to strengthen my patience."

Catherine smiled. "It's your fault. You started it."

Olivia reached down for Maya's pet carrier. "Let me walk you to your car before I don't give you the opportunity to leave."

Twenty-One

CATHERINE CAREFULLY PLACED THE TRAY holding her cup of lemon herbal tea and bowl of homemade chicken soup on her desk. She settled into her chair and tucked herself into her father's old mahogany desk. As a child she spent countless hours sitting in her father's lap as he tried patiently to explain the infinite rows of numbers he processed for the clients of his accounting firm. She could still remember the scent of his cigars that always sat in the crystal ashtray on the edge of his desk. She swiveled in her chair and smiled at the screen-saver image of her favorite photo of her parents. They looked so blissfully happy. Neither knowing that would be the last carefree photo taken of them together. Her father was diagnosed and died that same year. It was so hard to believe that was eight years ago.

She held the cup of tea in both hands and breathed in the fruity aroma. She leaned her head back against the rich leather and looked into her father's crystal blue eyes. "I wish you were here to meet Olivia, Dad. She's so incredible. But you know me and all my insecurities. I question everything. I wish you could tell me what to do. I just need a sign."

Catherine was jarred from her thoughts by a soft knock at her door. "Come in."

She swiveled in her chair and saw Olivia standing in the doorway. She stood. "Olivia! What are you doing here?"

"I told Ruth I needed to escape for a bit at lunch. I wanted to see you."

Olivia opened her arms and Catherine stepped into them, luxuriating in the intense heat of the embrace. She spread her hands wide, feeling the contours of Olivia's back through the plush suede of her jacket as the light scent of her perfume filled her senses.

She brushed her cheek against Olivia's before hesitantly stepping back and taking her hands. "Olivia, it's so important to me that we're open and honest with each other. I need to say this. I hate mind games and I would never do that to you. My body wanted what happened last night, intensely. I don't regret that kiss at all, but I'm not sure my heart was ready for it."

"I know that. And I respect your request for time. I'm not going to push you in any way, Catherine. I've made it perfectly clear that I want you. It's now up to you to decide what you want from me. I feel blessed to have your friendship. If that's all you give me I'll learn to live with it. But I want you in my life in whatever capacity you'll allow. No demands and no pressure. I came here this afternoon mainly to tell you that. Special Agent Laura even pointed me toward your office."

Olivia trailed her hands down Catherine's arms, squeezed her hands once, then let go. She looked with admiration around the spacious office, decorated beautifully in bright greens and gold. Catherine's forest green leather executive chair and large antique mahogany desk were nestled by a small window. Four filing cabinets filled one wall and a shelf of pictures and plants filled the opposite wall. A gold suede love seat sat nestled among four antique chairs. In the center of the circle of chairs sat an old wooden chest as a coffee table.

Olivia walked to Catherine's desk and picked up a small treasure chest sitting beside the computer. She balanced the treasure chest in the palm of her hand. "This must be the treasure chest you told me about, where you put all your dreams and wishes."

Catherine stood before her. "It is. I love treasure chests. I love their mystery and intrigue. The coffee table is an old chest my father's family has owned for six generations. The one you're holding is very special. My parents bought it for me in Dublin when we went on our first family vacation there. I was five at the time. That's where I put our fortunes from our fortune cookies."

Olivia placed the chest gently back in its rightful place. "Have you been following your heart lately?"

"I've been trying."

"Good girl." Olivia reached into the pocket of her jacket and pulled out a small emerald-silk purse-string pouch. She held the bag before Catherine and dropped it into her outstretched palm.

Catherine opened the pouch. She peeked inside then shook several puzzle pieces into the palm of her hand. She looked up at Olivia with a questioning frown.

"Every day for the next two weeks I'm going to give you thirty-six pieces to this puzzle. The puzzle has a total of five hundred pieces. The completed puzzle has a message for you that I'd like to convey. Once you put the puzzle together, we'll see if the message means the same to you as it does to me."

Catherine looked both pleased and perplexed. "I was never very good at puzzles. I wouldn't even know where to start, with so few pieces."

"The beginning's the hard part. But the pieces will keep coming. In the meantime, it's up to you how much time you want to see me. You know the demands on my time. I just want what's best for you."

Catherine returned the puzzle pieces to the pouch. "Right now, I don't want to let you go. But I convinced myself this morning that I need a few days without seeing you. That may be the only way I can put things in perspective. I think I need to honor that."

"Then I will, too. I know this has been an intense time for you, Catherine. You'll receive your puzzle pieces every day, but other than that you won't hear a word from me."

Catherine set the pouch on her desk, not yet ready for Olivia to leave. "Did Ruth make it home safely?"

"She did. I hear she has dinner plans with your mom this evening. I told her she absolutely has to come and pick up Abbott and Costello before midnight or I'll let them loose in the neighborhood. You can just imagine the barrage I heard then. I told her to bring Dana over after dinner and then she can take those two pains in my behind home with her. She agreed to that plan, thank God."

Catherine smiled. "Speaking of those two mischievous thrill seekers, how's your head feeling this morning?"

"Much better than last night. I can't tell you how much I'm looking forward to a ferret-free home."

"I can just imagine." She paused, not sure she was ready to ask her next question. "Wasn't your appointment with Emma today?"

"It was. I saw her in my office this morning. I think she'll do well. She's a real fighter."

Olivia held Catherine's gaze, waiting. Catherine took a breath and managed not to look away. She wanted to hear about Emma but felt fearful of any bad news. She felt Olivia begin to withdraw.

Olivia glanced at the small gold clock on Catherine's desk. "I should get going, unfortunately."

Catherine reached for her arm. "I honestly care about what happens to Emma, Olivia. I care about your work and your patients. I'm just always imaging the worst-case scenario. I don't know how much my heart can take of that. But I've got to try and get past my own fears. Please, tell me more about your appointment with Emma."

Olivia stepped closer and laid her hands gently on Catherine's shoulders. "I'm going to remove that lump for her. I've ordered her a series of preop tests. She said she's been feeling like her heart's racing lately so I'm sending her to see a cardiologist. Having a cardiologist for a housemate comes in handy—Echo was able to schedule her an appointment in three weeks. Hopefully she'll clear her for surgery."

Catherine stepped into Olivia's arms. "Emma just wanted a fighting chance, and that's what you're giving her. You're my hero."

"I like the stories where the hero gets the girl."

Unable to resist, Catherine touched her lips softly, slowly, and sensuously to Olivia's and felt immersed in her raspy, wanton moan. She stared into those sultry amber eyes. "I have no self-control when you hold me close. I hadn't meant to do that."

Olivia skimmed her thumb along Catherine's moist lower lip. "I'm glad you did."

Catherine sat on the love seat staring down at the puzzle pieces spread on her father's wooden chest. When the door opened, she looked up and smiled to see her mother. "What're you doing here on your day off? I thought you had a bunch of running around to do today."

Dana joined her daughter on the love seat. "Most of it's done already. I was in the area, so I thought I'd stop by and hear the details of the fiasco with Abbott and Costello. I kept visualizing all of you dashing around that bathroom trying to catch Ruth's beloved pets. Thank God she has no idea the kind of adventure they've had."

"You're not kidding."

Dana glanced down at the chest. "Is this a jigsaw puzzle?"

Catherine nodded. "Olivia stopped by the store at lunch-time. She gave me pieces to a puzzle she wants me to put together over the next two weeks. She's going to send me thirty-six new pieces every day. It sounded fun at first, but I can't make any sense of it."

"What a wonderful idea." Dana leaned closer and picked up one of the pieces. She laid the piece back on the chest and picked up another. "Look how beautiful this one is. It looks like part of the wing of a butterfly."

Catherine shook her head as she studied the puzzle pieces. Some of them showed lush foliage, others what seemed to be drapery.

"Look," Dana said. "This one's an edge piece. Let's put it off to the side. And this one has some sky in it, so we can put it near the top."

"You're much better at this than I am."

"Just be patient, darling. Every day you'll have new pieces to work with."

They tried the pieces in different positions as Catherine filled her mother in on the night before. "Would you like some of my homemade chicken soup? I pulled a big container out of the freezer and brought it in this morning."

"I'd love to have some of your soup, but I'm off to buy a new outfit for tonight. Nothing in my closet seems right for sushi."

Catherine tilted her head and looked closely at her mother. "You always say you have enough clothing in your closets to last several lifetimes. You don't usually worry about having something to wear."

"I know, but I feel like wearing something new." She stood, then leaned down and kissed her daughter. "Wish me luck in my shopping."

Catherine followed her mother out of the office, and watched her wave as she headed for the coffee shop. She leaned back against the doorframe, thinking she couldn't remember the last time her mother looked nervous about going out with a friend.

Twenty-Two

RUTH DROVE HER METALLIC BLUE Porsche Boxster onto
Dana's driveway and put it into park. She locked it with
the key remote and headed for the ornate pine front door, a
floral pattern etched in the half-moon window above it. This
was the third time she'd come to pick up Dana to take her
to dinner and each time she thought of how the house perfectly suited Dana and her personality. It was the house that
Catherine grew up in and Dana had shared with her husband.
The lawns and flowerbeds were always immaculately mani-
cured. It was a beautiful bungalow, with stone pillars and
sloped roofs. It gave an ambiance of welcoming warmth.

Ruth rang the doorbell and heard the deep resonant chime
that reminded her of church bells. The bolt slid on the door
and Dana appeared in the open doorway. She was stunning
in a purple-lined tank dress created in two flowing layers. It
didn't matter how many times Ruth reminded herself that
Dana was a straight girl. Her heart lurched and her chest felt
like it was filled with surging light every time she saw her.

"Welcome home, Ruth. Please come in."

That harmonic sweet voice always encompassed Ruth like
a warm embrace. "Thank you. It's wonderful to be home."

Dana closed the front door and kissed Ruth's cheek,
as she'd been doing over the past year when they'd gotten

together for dinner. Ruth inhaled her light flowery perfume before tentatively stepping back. "It's so good to see you. You're wearing that lovely plumeria scent."

Dana blushed. "I know how much you like that perfume, so I put it on for you." Dana touched a strand of light brown hair at Ruth's ear. "You got your hair cut shorter since you left for Phoenix."

Ruth ran her hand aimlessly across the top of her hair. "I did. I needed something different. What do you think?"

"I like it very much. The style suits you perfectly. Short and sassy."

Ruth placed her hands on her hips. "Are you calling me short?"

Dana smiled as she reached into the front closet and pulled out her cardigan. "Hardly. However, sassy suits you perfectly."

Ruth took the cardigan from Dana's hands and held it out for her. "You look absolutely radiant this evening, Mrs. O'Grady. I love that purple dress on you."

"Thank you. You look rather dashing yourself in that cream suit."

Ruth looked down at herself. "Thanks. I thought it gave me the sassy look I was going for."

Dana smiled as she reached for Ruth's arm and guided her out the front door. Ruth unlocked her Porsche and opened the passenger door.

Dana hesitated. "You do remember that we're picking up Abbott and Costello later?"

"How could I possibly forget? Olivia's reminded me at least a dozen times today. She even left a Post-it note on my windshield."

Dana laughed. "Then where do you propose to put them and all their stuff?"

Ruth gave her a charming smile. "I thought I could ask you to hold their pet carrier in your lap. All the rest of their stuff Olivia can bring to work tomorrow."

Dana rolled her eyes and slipped into the passenger seat. "What I won't do for you."

Ruth leaned against the open door. "That's what I was hoping you'd say. Besides, I wanted to take you somewhere before we head to dinner. The drive is so much nicer in my Porsche than my Expedition." Dana looked at her quizzically as she slowly closed her door.

Ruth maneuvered down the driveway and turned down the tree-lined street. "How's you mother?" Dana asked.

"She's getting better and stronger. They're getting her out of bed every day and she's taken several steps with a walker. She hates the thing but she needs the support while she learns to walk again. She's going to a rehab facility tomorrow for a couple of weeks and then she should be able to go home."

"I'm so happy to hear how well she's done."

"Me, too. She had me worried. But her strong spirit has made me proud."

Dana smiled. "Like mother, like daughter. How did it feel to get back to work?"

"It was wonderful. I had a lot of catching up to do on my patients and what has happened in the last week. Olivia and our other partners did a fabulous job in my absence. At our staff meeting today, I couldn't thank them all enough for covering for me. Olivia had the audacity to say that this week just showed them all how dispensable I was." Dana's laughter filled Ruth's soul. "We had a silicone model of the breast sitting on the table and I picked it up and threw it right at her.

It was pretty hilarious to see it bounce off her chest and land upright in her lap. Quite the odd anatomical image." Their laughter filled the car as Ruth negotiated the next curve.

Dana let the rich leather of the seat envelope her as Ruth sped north along Interstate 5. The drive along the winding coastal highway was exhilarating. The homes always seemed precariously balanced on the hillsides as the ocean collided with the land below. Brilliant, abstract streaks of deep orange-red stained the evening sky as Ruth exited Interstate 5 onto Torrey Pines Road in La Jolla.

Dana looked at Ruth as she expertly guided the sleek sports car along La Jolla Boulevard. She never quite understood why she felt so completely safe and at peace when she was with Ruth. She felt a bond with her that seemed ageless and precious.

Ruth saw an intensity and startling warmth in Dana's eyes. "Penny for your thoughts."

"I was just thinking how much I enjoy being with you. I was also wondering where you were taking me."

"We're going to close a chapter, Dana." Ruth guided the Porsche up the steep incline to Mount Soledad and pulled up beside an old Spanish church.

Dana was astounded by the huge, white-walled structure. The main building towered high into the sky with six massive bells suspended at the top. The small cemetery to the east was well kept with rows of simple white crosses as headstones. "I know you would never take me to church before feeding your tummy."

"You're so right about that."

Dana could hear the roar of the ocean as they walked across a well-manicured lawn and stopped at a rough-hewn wooden fence. Dana looked down at the jagged cliffs awash with foaming salt water. A group of seagulls cried out to their mates as they swooped onto a treacherous ledge. The abstract splash of red-orange dipped into the ocean beyond the horizon. The gentle breeze swirled the scent of the ocean around them. "This is such a beautiful spot. I've never been here before."

"I was hoping you'd like it." Ruth slipped her hand into the pocket of her cream blazer and pulled out a pill container. She held it out to Dana. "These are for you."

"What's this?"

"It's filled with pink breast-cancer M&M's. I was hoping we could pretend they were your Tamoxifen pills. I know you said you dreamed of getting to this five-year mark and finally being able to toss your pills in the ocean. I'd hate to see the dolphins and seals overdose on Tamoxifen so I filled the container with M&M's instead."

Ruth saw the tears glisten in Dana's eyes. She unscrewed the lid and shook the M&M's into Dana's hand. "When I was a kid my grandmother would always bring me to the beach by her house. I loved throwing shells back into the surf. She told me that every time you throw something back into the ocean you're supposed to make a wish. So now that you've accomplished your dream of making it to the five-year mark, you have to make a wish of what you want from your life from here on in."

Dana gently balanced the pink M&M's in the open palm of her hand. She stepped before Ruth and touched her face. "You're very special." She turned and faced the wooden fence and closed her eyes. She brushed away the tears on her cheeks and bowed her head. She stood stone still as the breeze flirted with the layers of her purple dress. Moments later she raised her head. She took one step back and took one M&M from the pile before tossing the rest high into the sky. They both looked down and watched each chocolate treat plop into the raging surf.

Ruth stood close beside her. "What did you wish for?"

"I took the liberty of making a wish for each M&M you gave me. I wish for continuing good health for myself and everyone I love. I wish to walk in the Susan G. Komen Race for the Cure as long as I can. I wish to visit the Vatican. I want to take a hot-air-balloon ride. I'd like to go back and visit Ireland. I want to see the bookstore continue growing in its success. I want to see Catherine in a happy relationship."

She turned to Ruth. "I've wished for five years for this time to come. It's here and you've made it so special. So I didn't need to toss in this last M&M to make that wish." Dana took the last M&M and held it before Ruth's mouth. She slipped it in between her parted lips and was jolted by the heat soaring through her at that simple touch. "My breast cancer enriched my life in so many ways. I feel so blessed that it's gone and you're here to stay."

Twenty-Three

RUTH DROVE HER PORSCHE beneath the Spanish arch-way and parked by the front doors. She unclipped her seat belt and smiled at the astonished look on Dana's face. "Gorgeous, isn't it?"

"Oh my, yes. Catherine told me about Olivia's home but this is truly spectacular."

Ruth walked around the car and opened Dana's door for her. She held out her hand and watched Dana's long, slender, shapely legs slip out of her seat.

"I saw some amazing homes during my twenty-five years as a real-estate agent, but this is staggering."

"Wait till you see the inside."

"I can't wait."

Ruth guided Dana through the front door and into the spacious foyer. Dana stared up at the domed stained-glass ceiling and blinked several times. "It's so beautiful."

"Well, you finally made it. I was just about to spring Abbott and Costello loose."

Ruth and Dana turned as Olivia walked toward them.

"You do that and you're fired," Ruth said. "Besides, you said I had till midnight and it's only nine."

Dana slipped into Olivia's warm embrace. "Your home is stunning."

"Thank you. I'm so glad to finally have you here. How was the sushi?"

"Excellent. The company was equally wonderful."

"I'm just grateful that Ruth has someone to drag out to raw fish besides me."

Dana turned to see two beautiful women walk toward her.

"Have you met Zoë and Echo?" Olivia said.

"I haven't had the pleasure. But I've seen them in our bookstore. It's lovely to see you both again. Catherine told me your daughter's due in eight weeks. How exciting."

"We can't wait," Zoë said.

"I hope you had less traffic traipsing through your bathroom this evening."

Echo smiled. "We had a very peaceful evening for a change."

"Haven't they finished your bathroom yet?" Ruth asked.

"Finishing touches should be done tomorrow. We're getting a little tired of the horde of men who've been coming and going through there. Come on up and we'll show you what they've done so far."

"I'd love a tour of this palatial home," Dana said.

Ruth looked through to the living room. "Can I say hello to Abbott and Costello first?"

"They're sound asleep on their favorite pillow. Let's do the tour and then you can get them all riled up again."

Echo took Dana and Ruth on a guided tour of the entire house and ended in the living room. Zoë poured everyone a cup of tea as Echo pointed at the pile of fur nestled peacefully on a huge pillow by the roaring fire.

"Oh, look at my babies. They look so content." Ruth headed for her beloved ferrets, kneeled down by their pillow, and started rubbing their heads. Abbott and Costello looked up at her and bounded into her arms.

Dana squeezed Echo's arm. "How in the world did you manage to get them to look so peaceful at such a perfect time?"

"I put them on the treadmill for twenty minutes and let them wear themselves out. They love it."

Dana laughed behind her hand. Echo joined Olivia and Zoë on the couch. Ruth sat on the floor caressing her pets, then pulled at something stuck in Abbott's fur and examined it carefully between her fingers. "Why are there bits of plaster stuck in their fur?"

The silence in the room was deafening. Everyone stared at Ruth as she placed Abbott and Costello back on the pillow and stood tall. "All right, who's going to tell me what happened?"

No one answered. Ruth reached into the brass holder beside the fireplace and grabbed the wrought-iron poker. The three housemates scattered. Dana reached for the poker and took it from Ruth's hands. The girls huddled together behind the couch.

Dana laid her hand on Ruth's waist. "Abbott and Costello got into Echo and Zoë's vanity and wouldn't come out. Catherine and Olivia brought Maya over and she flushed them out. End of story. A little plaster never hurt a ferret, did it?"

Ruth grabbed a bunch of pillows and threw them across the room at the girls. They screamed and dove behind the couch.

Dana grabbed Ruth's arms. "Stop it. You should be ashamed of yourself for throwing pillows anywhere near a pregnant woman."

Zoë popped her head up from behind the couch. "Yeah, you should be ashamed."

Dana touched Ruth's face. "Nobody intended for Abbott and Costello to get stuck in the vanity, and nobody was hurt. Well, maybe just Olivia's head when she smacked it against the toilet bowl and the wall trying to get Abbott."

Ruth stepped away and threw her arms in the air. "I don't believe you guys. I trusted you with the well-being of my Abbott and Costello. How could you let them get into the vanity and then send a cat after them? They were probably terrified. I'm amazed they didn't keel over and die with fright." She turned to Dana. "And you knew this happened and you didn't tell me?"

"I just told you."

"Yeah, after I had a weapon in my hand."

Dana motioned to the ferrets. "Look at those two. Do they look any worse for wear? You should just be grateful that the girls were all kind enough to care for your pets on such short notice so you could go be with your mother."

Olivia peeked around the edge of the couch. "Yeah, you should be grateful."

Ruth threw her an icy stare. "This from a woman who called me dispensable at our staff meeting today."

Olivia threw a pillow right back at her. "You threw a breast in my lap."

The girls burst into laughter. Dana wished Catherine were here to share in the fun. She found herself believing her daughter *belonged* here, in this warm, wonderful house filled with so much love.

She cautiously took Ruth's hands. "You know better than most that there are so many worse things in life than having your ferrets take up hiding in someone's vanity."

Ruth looked down at their hands. "How can I stay angry when you put it like that?"

"That's the point. It's not worth it. All is well and you have your beloved ferrets back in one piece."

"I'm still not happy that you didn't tell me this sooner."

"Why would I do that? I had no intention of ruining a great sushi dinner. Besides, someone was supposed to give those two a bath and dispose of the plaster evidence."

The girls started pointing wildly at each other. Ruth folded her arms across her chest. "So, you were going to hide the evidence and not even tell me about this if I didn't find the plaster myself."

"That was the game plan," Olivia admitted.

Ruth looked back at Dana. "So what else are you hiding from me?"

Dana gazed intently into Ruth's eyes. "I've never been able to hide anything from you. That bothers me more than anything."

Ruth skimmed her fingertips across Dana's cheek and gathered her in her arms.

Echo and Zoë looked at each other and widened their eyes in surprise. Olivia spoke quietly. "That's quite a hug."

Twenty-Four

Laura zipped up her sweater, marveling at the pure joy on her children's faces. Their concentration was fierce as they carefully followed Catherine's directions in the construction of their moat. They filled pail after pail of fine beige beach sand and tossed it aside to establish a waterway around their elegant castle. Catherine placed cocktail toothpicks in each turret; Amanda stood and watched the tide fill their moat, and Sean placed a small American flag at the portal to the main entrance.

Laura dug her painted toes into the cool beach sand. It was a beautiful warm March morning, promising to leave the rainy season behind. Laura loved bringing her kids to this spot on Mission Beach. You truly had the sense of being on a narrow peninsula with the Pacific Ocean spread before you and Mission Bay behind. The paved boardwalk showcased many colorful people zipping by on wheels of all kinds or bravely strolling along. A people-watcher's paradise. The pastel-colored homes and condos crowded the boardwalk, vying for their claim of prime real estate.

Catherine leaned back on her heels and examined their work. "Now, that is one fine castle, fit for Prince Sean and Princess Amanda." They all applauded the masterpiece.

Sean grabbed his boogey board. "Come on, Amanda. Let's go surfing."

"Stay in close," Laura called to her children as they ran into the gentle surf. "I don't want you going out too far."

"We will, Mom," Amanda called back.

Catherine picked up their pails and shovels and placed them beside the cooler. She brushed the sand off her legs. "How do you keep up with those two?"

"It's a challenge most days, trust me."

Catherine eased onto the big Mexican blanket beside Laura and gladly accepted the bottle of water. "Thank you. I'm parched."

"You know, I'm not sure who has more fun building those huge sandcastles, you or them."

Catherine smiled. "It brings back such fond memories of when I was a kid. My dad taught me everything I know about sandcastle architecture."

Laura kept a watchful eye on her children as she hugged her knees in tight. "I remember the day we tossed his ashes into the ocean like it was yesterday."

"Me, too. I always feel a connection to him when I look out at the Pacific. It's a nice feeling."

They sat together in comfortable silence as Amanda chased her Barbie boogey board along the gentle swells tumbling toward the shore.

"Did you decide how soon you want to see Olivia?" Laura asked.

Catherine brushed a spot of sand off her ankle. "I talked to her yesterday. We decided to go on a hike together on Sunday. It's only been three days since we saw each other, and I feel like there's a big hole in my life. It doesn't make sense. I want time away from her, and I need to be with her."

"I don't think love is supposed to make sense."

"Is this love, Laura? I don't know what it is I'm looking for, or what sign I'm waiting for, to feel confident about Olivia. I think I'm terrified of getting close to Olivia for fear of losing her like I lost Alexis and Kayla. I keep dwelling on the obstacles between us, but it's more than that."

"You were just as cautious with Alexis before you committed to her."

"Look where that got me."

"My point is I thought you and Alexis were a perfect couple. Who could have ever predicted she would betray you like that?"

"What could I have done to prevent it?"

"Absolutely nothing. It was Alexis's choice. Unfortunately, it destroyed you and Kayla. You've spent the past two years picking yourself up and rebuilding your life. Now Olivia has come to you. You've had a rocky start, yet you both care so much for each other. I've only spoken to her that one time at the store. But I saw the way she looks at you. I watched the way she talks to you. I saw the look in her eyes when I blasted her for upsetting you. She cares deeply for you. There is no such thing as reassurances when it comes to relationships, Catherine. You know that. All you can do is go with your gut feeling and follow your heart."

Catherine shook her head. "Why are you supporting Olivia all of sudden? You're the one who wanted to commit her to the gallows."

"I'm not exactly ready to commit to her, either. I just want you to be happy. I don't want you to be completely tainted by your heartache with Alexis. Besides, my gut tells me she has potential. My gut's never wrong. Don't you dare tell her I said that."

Catherine laughed. "Olivia would be shocked by your support."

"Good." Laura sipped from her water bottle and watched her children courageously prance in the cold water. "I had a dream about you last night."

Catherine lowered her sunglasses and stared at Laura. "What was it about?"

"We were here building sandcastles with my kids and yours. Yours and Olivia's."

Tears misted Catherine's eyes. "Girls or boys?"

"Two beautiful little girls. Not as cute as my kids, but almost."

Catherine looked out to sea, fighting back tears, trying to decide how much to tell her friend. "That's the other thing, Laura. A big one. I don't think Olivia wants children. She's excited about being an aunt, but I don't think she wants children of her own."

Laura put her arm around Catherine. "There's so much you still have to discover about each other, Catherine. And about yourselves. Don't let your fear keep you from that discovery."

Dana watched Catherine weave her way through the coffee shop. "How was your morning on the beach?" she asked.

Catherine embraced her mother. "It was great. Laura is such a good friend."

Dana reached around for a bundle of mail secured with a thick rubber band. "She always has been. Here's your mail. I put the lumpiest letter on top for you."

Catherine pulled the letter out and frowned. "I can't believe this. Olivia's sending these packages Express. It's a ridiculous waste of money."

"Not if it makes her happy. Olivia has wealth from her family, darling, and she makes good money now. I think you need to accept that as part of who she is."

"Easier said than done." Catherine shook the package and heard the puzzle pieces rattling around. "This makes for a hundred and forty-four puzzle pieces total. Let's go see if more of them will finally fit."

"I'd love to. It's pretty quiet right now."

They retreated to Catherine's office. Dana slipped into a chair and studied the puzzle pieces scattered across the old chest. "Look at this. You've made progress with the border."

Catherine settled into a chair beside Dana and laid the envelope in her lap. "I'm not doing as well with the middle."

Dana picked up a piece of greenery and snapped it together with another, then joined two pieces of drapery. "So open that envelope."

Catherine laughed. "You're more excited than I am about putting this thing together."

"Yes, I am. And I'm going to have a few words with that Dr. Olivia Carrington for dragging it on like this."

Catherine tore open the envelope and let the pieces scatter on the old chest. "I wish you would."

They leaned in close together and sorted each piece face up. One of the pieces immediately caught Catherine's eye. She picked it up, searching for another piece she'd noticed the day before. She joined the two. "Look at this. It's a woman's face."

"Isn't she beautiful!" Dana moved her matched pieces of drapery over beneath the face. "And this is probably her dress. Oh, and look darling, this isn't a butterfly wing at all, it belongs to the woman. I think she's a fairy."

They worked silently trying to match colors and patterns. Catherine carefully analyzed a corner piece, then decided to place it at the bottom left. "Laura thinks I should lighten up my scrutiny of Olivia."

"That's a big leap of faith for Laura. What do you think?"

"I think my concerns are valid."

"Then don't lighten up. Do what you think is right. I believe you'll make the right decision when you're ready."

"How patient do you think Olivia can be?"

"If you're what she's wants, she'll wait till you're ready. That'll be one of the tests of your love. It's always been important to you to test the people in your life and know that they're worthy of your undying devotion."

"You make me sound horrible."

"Far from it, darling. It's important to you to know that the people near and dear to you have substance. When that's been proven to you, you give back one hundred and fifty percent."

Catherine stared at the vibrant puzzle pieces, trying to will them into a form she could understand. Her mother seemed far more convinced than she was that she and Olivia would be together in the end. She snapped another piece into place. "It's not that I doubt her substance, Mom. It's just that I'm not sure we're right for each other."

"You're cautious about everything in life, darling. Your relationships especially. There's nothing wrong with that. You're only protecting your heart."

Twenty-Five

OLIVIA SLIPPED ON HER KNAPSACK. "This is the beginning of the Guy Fleming trail. Are you ready?"

"Wait just a minute," Catherine said, pointing to a warning about rattlesnakes posted on the message board at the trailhead. "I'm really not interested in seeing any reptiles on this hike."

Olivia laughed. "You're such a city girl. It's not hot enough for the snakes to be out on the trail. Besides, they're more afraid of you than you are of them. If we do see one, just stay back and give it ample room to slither away."

Olivia had picked her up an hour before, outside the bookstore. It had been so easy, so natural. Catherine had expected her heart to jump, seeing Olivia for the first time in five days, but mostly she'd felt a pure sense of comfort and belonging, and they'd talked so easily on the drive up to the trailhead. Right now, however, she wished they'd decided on a shopping expedition, rather than a hike.

"That's it, I'm leaving." She turned to head back down the trail.

Olivia dashed after her and grabbed her arm. "I'm just teasing, Catherine. You won't see any snakes. It's too early in the morning. Stick with me and I'll keep you safe. Besides,

147

if by some small chance one nips at your toes through those girly-girl sandals, I know a toxicologist."

"That's comforting."

Olivia took Catherine's hand and started up the trail, feeling her own heart expand in this familiar place. Within minutes she felt Catherine's grip relax as a gentle breeze cooled them from the ocean and the sound of the surf propelled them forward. The narrow, flat trail wound through a dense area of pines and opened out onto a carpet of purple and yellow wildflowers. The view never ceased to amaze Olivia, the explosion of vibrant color spilling down the cliffs.

"That's truly beautiful," Catherine said.

Olivia picked one of the bright orange California poppies and tucked it behind Catherine's ear. "March is always the perfect time of year to see the wildflowers out here. We just need to go a little further down the trail and I can show you one of the famed Torrey pines growing out of the edge of the sandstone cliffs."

The way the Torrey pines managed to anchor themselves in the craggy rocks and bend to the demands of the fierce coastal winds always moved Olivia. Every time she looked at them, she was inspired by their tenacity, ingenuity, and survival.

They continued on, to a view of the trees. "They're so beautiful," Catherine said. "How can they live so precariously?"

"I don't know. But sometimes when I feel alone or overwhelmed I think of these pines out here in the elements, teetering on a rocky ledge, and I draw on their strength and endurance." Catherine turned to her, her eyes full of compassion. "Come on, we're almost at the North Overlook."

They stepped onto the platform and looked down onto Torrey Pines State Beach. They could see people playing in the surf and walking along the sandy shores. A group of pelicans proudly stood guard on the craggy rocks, scouting their next meal. Olivia dug into her knapsack and handed Catherine a bottle of water. The look of astonishment on Catherine's face gave Olivia deep pleasure.

"This is an incredible view," Catherine said.

Olivia took a sip of water. "We're two hundred and fifty feet above sea level." She pointed to the north. "That's the Peñasquitos Lagoon and Del Mar. We'll walk to the South Overlook next, where on a clear day like today you can see La Jolla, San Clemente, and Catalina Islands. I've seen dolphins from that spot. I love going there in the winter to see the gray whales during their migration. It's truly amazing."

"I can imagine. How often do you come up here?"

"I make an effort to do these trails once a month. I wish it could be more often."

"It's easy to see why you would enjoy this. The view is stunning in it's raw beauty and power. It feels very spiritual up here."

"Yeah, it's about as close to God as I can get."

"Even though you joke about it, this place is obviously very special to you and must give you some sense of a higher power."

"Maybe not a higher power, but certainly a sense of peace. This spot right here is my place of worship. When I come here, I can just be. I don't have to give, just take. I come here to recharge my solar panels and rejoice in something that's much bigger than me and all my worries. I find I can bare my soul and shed my tears and find strength in all this beauty. I always leave here with a better perspective on what's really important in life."

"Which is?"

"Family, love, a home, and a job that I love."

Catherine brushed her fingertips across Olivia's cheek. "You have a much stronger faith than even you know."

Twenty-Six

O N MONDAY AFTERNOON, Catherine glanced across the crowded coffee shop just as her mother guided a young woman to the only empty table, then headed to the coffee-shop counter. The woman sat very stiffly on the edge of her seat and took a deep breath as if to force herself to relax. Catherine watched her mother head back to the table with a hot cup of coffee. Catherine stepped down from the customer-service desk and headed for their table.

"Just the girl I was hoping to see," Dana said. "Natalie, this is my daughter, Catherine. Catherine, I'd like you to meet Natalie."

Natalie took Catherine's hand. "Hi. It's nice to meet you. Your mother's been a real source of comfort to me this week."

"She has that amazing gift."

Dana smiled sweetly. "Can you join us, dear?"

Catherine hesitated a moment then took a seat.

"Natalie's mother is one of Olivia's patients. She had a mastectomy ten days ago for grade-three breast cancer. I've met a few times with Natalie to offer her some motherly support."

Catherine realized this must be the young woman Olivia had told her about, the night they argued on the phone. She remembered that Natalie's mother was only forty-eight.

She could only imagine what the two of them were going through. "I'm really sorry to hear about your mom."

Tears filled Natalie's eyes, and Dana handed her a tissue from the pocket of her slacks. "She finally got out of the ICU a few days ago, and is doing much better today, so I thought I'd steal Natalie away and treat her to a coffee."

"That's a wonderful idea. Just sitting in that hospital is enough to depress anyone."

Natalie blew her nose. "It is. Dana told me about her surgery and how you were there with her every day. It's just been really hard. I think I'm doing better, and then I fall apart. It's not just the breast cancer. Mom got pneumonia because she wasn't breathing right, plus she's diabetic and we've had problems with her blood sugar. Now that it's under control, I'm back to facing her breast cancer."

Catherine noticed several customers standing at the customer-service desk, and was surprised at how reluctant she felt to leave Natalie. She truly understood what this young woman was going through. She didn't have the strength to visit cancer patients in the hospital the way her mother did, but maybe she could help another daughter.

She looked at her mother. "Mom, one of us should take care of those customers. Do you mind?"

Dana smiled. "That would be my pleasure."

Catherine turned back to Natalie. "My mother was never in the ICU, but I certainly can understand how awful this must be for you. I was terrified the whole time she was in the hospital and just wanted to get her out of there and take her home. That way at least there was a semblance of normal life."

"Exactly. I'm so afraid of what this all means. My mother lives alone and I don't know if I should be making arrangements for her to come live with me. I don't know if I should be taking time off work to be with her once she leaves the hospital and starts chemotherapy. It may sound selfish, but I need to know how this is going to affect my life as well."

"I understand. Your world has been flipped upside down."

Natalie gripped the coffee in both hands. "Yes, it has. My mom and I have always been close. Since her diagnosis I don't know how to act, what to do, what to say or how to help. I have so many questions, but I'm terrified of the answers."

"I know how you feel. But I found my fear of the unknown was so much worse than the reality of the situation. Mom and I wrote down all our questions for Dr. Ratcliff, because at the time neither one of us could think straight. That really helped."

"Dr. Carrington has been great with my mother, but I'm having a real hard time talking to her and absorbing everything she tells me. I know it's my fear talking, but I just shut down."

"Believe me, I know how easy it is to see doctors as the enemy, but I think right now Dr. Carrington may be your biggest ally. I know when my mother and I had our questions answered, we both began to feel stronger and more in control. It made an amazing difference in our attitudes and determination to be survivors." Catherine could see the spark of hope in the young woman's eyes.

"I want to beat this. I'm not ready to lose my mother. I don't want to be wasting my time wallowing in my fears. I want to know what to do and how to do it."

Catherine smiled. "Why don't we begin by writing down all your questions for Dr. Carrington? I might be able to add some from what I've learned from my mother's experience. How does that sound?"

Natalie pushed her coffee aside. "That sounds wonderful."

Twenty-Seven

CATHERINE SET THE DISHWASHER TO RUN and wiped down the kitchen counters for a second time. She couldn't think of any thing else she could do to keep her mind occupied. The laundry was done, the trash was out for the next morning, and she still felt too antsy to sit and enjoy a cup of tea.

Olivia had been true to her word about allowing Catherine to initiate any contact, allowing her the time she needed to figure out her feelings. Catherine adored her for her patience. Then why did she feel so restless when they hadn't talked in a day? She was becoming frustrated by her own rules and boundaries.

Catherine had called Olivia on Monday morning to thank her for the amazing hike on Sunday and to chastise her for sending a private courier to the bookstore to deliver Sunday's thirty-six puzzle pieces. She had truly enjoyed their conversation, but decided not to call on Tuesday. It was now Wednesday evening and quickly approaching ten o'clock.

Catherine walked through her living room and couldn't believe she wished she had that damn puzzle at home with her. What had started off as a source of frustration had turned into a lovely challenge. Whenever she spent time with the puzzle she felt such a comfortable connection with Olivia. She needed that now.

She thought back to this afternoon, when she'd shaken the puzzle pieces from their envelope. She'd become fond of the beautiful fairy taking shape on the antique chest, though aspects of her form and clothing weren't falling into place. Today, among the new puzzle pieces, Catherine had found a second lovely face. At first she'd been taken aback, needing to rearrange her mental image of the picture as a whole. Then she'd rearranged the pieces—the blue drapery for this figure, the cream drapery for that one—to reveal the emerging forms of not one but two ethereal fairies, facing each other.

Catherine slipped into her cream cabled cardigan and grabbed the cordless phone, then stepped out onto her back patio and admired the beautiful moon. She wondered if Olivia was enjoying the same moon. *Are you on your patio with a glass of orange juice sitting by your fire pit? Or are you getting ready for bed after another busy day at the hospital?*

Catherine needed to stop analyzing and dissecting. She dialed Olivia's cell phone.

"Well, isn't this a lovely surprise."

Catherine slipped into an Adirondack chair. "I hope it wasn't too late to call, Olivia."

"Not at all."

"What are you doing?"

"I was just thinking about mowing the lawn."

"Olivia, it's ten o'clock at night."

"I have to do something productive to get you off my mind."

"Do you have headlights on your lawn mower?"

"I've never operated a lawn mower in my life. Do they come with headlights?"

Catherine laughed. "Here I thought I was the one unable to get a woman off my mind."

"Nice to hear that, my Irish friend."

"I wanted to tell you about meeting Natalie on Monday. A meeting my mother totally orchestrated."

Olivia laughed. "Your mother told me about her plot. How did it go?"

"Actually, really well. I understand what she's going through. We compiled a list of questions for you. Brace yourself."

"God help me. I really do appreciate you taking the time with her, Catherine. Her fear is pulling her away from her mother, who needs her more now than ever. I'll answer her questions and hopefully make her feel like an important part of her mother's recovery."

"I know you will. You're not the big bad enemy after all."

"I'm so glad you at least have realized that."

Catherine skimmed her thumb around the edge of her glass. "I was wondering if you had any plans for dinner tomorrow night?"

"Actually, I do. Echo's a grill master. She promised to barbecue Zoë and me a couple of steaks. Why don't you join us?"

"I'd love to join you for barbecued steaks. What can I bring?"

"Absolutely nothing. Just your wonderful self."

"It's the Irish way to bring something, so I'll bring wine. How does that sound?"

"You certainly don't need to, but who am I to interfere in the rituals of an Irish woman."

"You're a fast learner, Dr. Carrington. Still feel like mowing the lawn?"

"Oh, no. I'm ready for a dreamy sleep now that I've heard your voice and will be seeing you tomorrow. Has this helped you as well?"

"Tremendously."

"Good then. Maybe you'll make a habit of it."

Catherine arrived at the front door of 25 Carriage House Lane to find a note taped to the front door.

Dear Catherine,

No need to knock! Come find me in the kitchen.

Love,
Echo

Catherine made her way through the glass-domed foyer and spacious family room to the sun-filled kitchen, where Echo was flipping steaks in a zesty-smelling marinade. Catherine set a brown grocery bag on the granite marble top. "Something smells great."

Echo looked up and smiled. "Well, hello there. Don't you look beautiful in that pink dress, Ms. Cocoa Cream."

"Thank you. The chef is looking rather chic herself. Thank you for inviting me to dinner, Echo."

"It's our pleasure. We're just glad you could come." Echo peeked into the grocery bag. "Olivia said you wanted to bring wine but she didn't say you were bringing the whole wine store."

"I brought four different kinds because I didn't know what you guys liked with your steak. That way we can have a variety. I also brought a jug of milk for Zoë. Olivia told me what kind she drinks."

Echo laughed. "You're too sweet."

"What can I do to help with dinner?"

"You can help by getting Olivia out of the pool. You two are on salad duty tonight."

Catherine smiled. "That would be my pleasure. Where's Zoë?"

"She's just getting up from her nap. Now, I'll put the milk away and pop the cork on this bottle of Merlot while you get the mermaid out of the pool. Tell her the lettuce will start wilting soon if you two don't start slicing and dicing. I want both of you back here in fifteen minutes or I'm serving you bloody steaks."

"Yuck."

Echo pointed down the hall, and Catherine headed toward the south end of the house. This place was filled with so much activity and life. She felt happy to be here, at home.

She stopped at the large double French doors and stared in wonderment. Olivia was slicing through the water with grace and agility, wearing a shiny gold swimsuit that clung to her shapely body like a second skin. The muscles of Catherine's belly clenched as she stepped through the doors.

Entering the large glassed-in solarium was like stepping into a rainforest. Multicolored pots of ferns hung seemingly free floating from the ceiling while fichus trees decorated all four corners of the room. Plush patio furniture lined one wall, giving an air of a resort. Catherine walked along the length of the lap pool, keeping in step with Olivia's long strokes.

Olivia smiled at her as she turned her head to take a deep breath. She hit the end of the pool and executed a perfect underwater turn and swam to the other side.

Catherine stepped out of her pink leather bow sandals. She held onto the hem of her dress as she stepped down onto the first step and sat on a plush plum towel. The warm water lapped against her calves as she wiggled her toes in the soothing water. She watched Olivia turn at the other end of the pool and head toward her. She extended her leg and Olivia reached forward and grabbed her foot.

Olivia dunked herself beneath the water and threw her head back. She resurfaced between Catherine's feet and brushed the water out of her eyes. She gripped Catherine's calves in her hands and stood before her. "Give me one good reason why I shouldn't pull you into this water with me?"

Catherine couldn't take her eyes away from Olivia's firm breasts straining against the shiny gold material. "Echo says we're on salad duty and we better get in the kitchen in exactly fifteen minutes or she's serving us bloody steaks."

"That's a good one. Give me another."

"I don't have a change of clothing."

"I'll respect that. Let this be a warning to you, however. Next time you sit before me looking so damn sexy, I can't promise I won't pull you into this pool."

"Is that a threat, Dr. Carrington?"

"No, ma'am, not at all. I'm just careful about what promises I make, and if I make them, I keep them. Including the promise to order a hundred candles for your beloved Father O'Brien. I even went in and met him personally, so I could find out who his supplier was."

Catherine leaned forward and placed her hands on Olivia's chest. "Did you really?"

"I sure did. Father O'Brien's a fascinating man. He had a lot of questions about you and me. I felt like your father was quizzing me. I mean that biologically."

Catherine laughed. She was also very touched that Olivia had taken time from her busy schedule to meet Father O'Brien.

"Between him and Laura, you should feel well protected from mean people and dangerous lesbians. He told me that you and your mother are very special to him and that you're both in his prayers every day. He said he prays you'll find a woman who will make you happy. He obviously knows about your lifestyle. I'm surprised he's so supportive."

Catherine smiled. "He's a darling man. He told me he doesn't understand homosexuality but that doesn't mean he's going to stop praying for all of his parishioners, regardless of their orientation. That's pretty open minded for a man of the cloth, don't you think?"

"Definitely. I'm very impressed."

"Does this mean you'll be coming to church with me next?"

Olivia skimmed her fingertips down Catherine's calves and became more serious. "I'll never believe what you believe, Catherine. But I want to understand what makes you who you are."

Catherine slowly leaned forward and brushed her lips lightly against Olivia's. Olivia let out a throaty groan and took Catherine's wet lips with a voracious yearning. Catherine met her stroke for stroke as she fed a longing she couldn't hold back.

Catherine leaned her face against Olivia's and struggled to catch her next breath. "Would Echo really feed us bloody steaks if we didn't show in fifteen minutes?"

"Never. It's just an empty threat. However, since you don't have a change of clothing we better get into that kitchen before I get you all wet."

Catherine slid her hands along Olivia's neck and held her face gently in her hands. "Too late."

Olivia smiled broadly.

Twenty-Eight

CATHERINE COMPLETED THE FINAL ENTRIES in her computer for the bookstore's electronic payroll and sent the information to the bank. She swiveled in her chair, slipped the copies of the time clock information into her payroll file, and placed it in the tray on her desk.

She looked across the room at the puzzle on her father's chest. The magnificent picture was nearly complete, a mystic forest with two lovely fairies facing each other in midflight. Scattered throughout the scene, the dark wood of the chest showed through where thirty-two pieces were missing. Today, she would fit those final pieces into place.

Catherine leaned back in her chair, thinking about this past weekend and how close she'd felt to Olivia. They'd met for lunch on Saturday. Yesterday they'd taken another hike, this time to Lake Hodges, and afterward Catherine had prepared an Irish feast of roast beef and Yorkshire pudding in her tiny kitchen. They'd eaten in her living room before a roaring fire. It was the longest they'd ever spent together, and Catherine hadn't wanted the day to end. Olivia was the one who had insisted it was time for her to head home.

Catherine closed her eyes and took a deep breath. Her head continued to question the very possibility of Dr. Carrington being the one, yet every day Olivia tugged her heartstrings a little tighter and a little closer.

A soft knock sounded at the door.

"Come in."

Laura opened the door and stepped into the office. "A bike courier just came by with a package for Catherine O'Grady. I'd bet my kids' college funds you've been waiting for it to arrive."

"Your kids' college funds are safe," Catherine said, smiling. She rose from her chair and took the package from Laura, turning it over in her hands. "I'm not even angry at Olivia for paying for a courier. I'm ready to see what this picture looks like when it's complete."

Catherine tore open the envelope and shook its contents onto the old chest. One of the puzzle pieces was wrapped in tissue paper. Olivia had written "Save me for last" across it in her careful script.

Catherine and Laura turned the other pieces face up and began fitting them into place. This ritual had become easier as the days had gone by and the picture had taken shape. Some days, Laura or Dana had helped Catherine with the puzzle; other days, she'd worked on it alone. Today, it was as if each piece was ready to leap into the gap in the beautiful scene waiting to receive it.

Catherine and Laura traded pieces back and forth, working in companionable silence. Catherine felt happy as the familiar figures of the fairies became complete, their lovely swirling dresses, the magical forest. Finally, no piece remained but the wrapped one. One fairy was handing the other what looked like a gold chain. The final piece would reveal the exact nature of the gift.

Laura handed Catherine the tissue-wrapped puzzle piece. Catherine carefully unwrapped it, her heart pounding unexpectedly. Confusion and emotion washed through her as she took in its meaning.

Laura studied the puzzle piece. "It's a pendant for the chain, isn't it? It's beautiful. It must mean something to you."

Catherine nodded. "It does. It's a Celtic four-pointed knot. It signifies eternity. It has no beginning and no end. It represents eternal beauty and conveys a message of love everlasting."

Laura put her hand on Catherine's shoulder. "I've prayed every day that you would find someone special to share your life. I can't tell you how happy it makes me to see that prayer being answered. You deserve the best, Catherine. I think you've finally found the woman who deserves you. But don't you dare tell her I said that."

Catherine squeezed Laura's hand. "Why do I still feel confused?"

"It wouldn't be love if it weren't confusing. Now, I better get back to work. Give that big mean doctor of yours a call and tell her your puzzle's complete."

"I will. But first I need a little time for things to sink in."

"I'm guessing that Olivia will be patient." Laura smiled as she headed out of the office.

Catherine placed the final piece into the green silk pouch Olivia had given her with the first pieces. She laid it on the puzzle before rising from her seat.

It had been three and a half weeks since she'd first set eyes on Olivia, that tumultuous day at the hospital, and now she was close to offering her her heart. Was it even possible to know in such a short time if love might be forever? How could Olivia have been so certain about her feelings two weeks ago, when she'd handed the first puzzle pieces to Catherine?

How could she have been so confident that Catherine would feel the same way, once the puzzle was complete?

Catherine's cell phone rang as she was deep in her thoughts. She looked at the unfamiliar number on the small screen. "Hello."

"Hello, I'm trying to reach Catherine O'Grady."

"This is Catherine. To whom am I speaking?"

"I'm a nurse in the emergency department at Children's Hospital. Do you know Kayla Blair?"

Catherine thought her chest would implode as she gripped her cell phone. "Yes, I do. What happened? Is she all right?"

"She will be. Her class was on a field trip to the Wild Animal Park when their school bus went off the road and hit a tree. Kayla has a pretty big bump on her head but she should be just fine. We need to keep her overnight for observation. The school's trying to reach her mother. Kayla asked me to call you."

Catherine clutched at her chest. "Please tell Kayla that I love her and I'm on my way."

"Okay Catherine, I will."

Catherine looked at the antique clock on her desk. She hit a preset button on her cell phone and paced frantically.

"Hello, my Irish girl. How are you?"

"Olivia, I'm scared. I just got a phone call from a nurse in the emergency department at Children's Hospital. Kayla's class was on a field trip and there was a bus accident. She has a bad bump on her head and she asked the nurse to call me. I'm heading right over."

Olivia didn't hesitate. "Would you like me to meet you there?"

"I'd really like that."

"Will you be okay to drive down by yourself?"

"Talking to you has calmed me. I'm just really shaken that Kayla's hurt and that she asked them to call me."

"I completely understand. Stay as calm as you can. Kayla needs you to be calm. Go to her. I'll be there soon."

Twenty-Nine

CATHERINE RUSHED THROUGH the double automatic sliding glass doors. She stopped breathlessly at the information desk. "I'm Catherine O'Grady. I'm looking for Kayla Blair."

The young Hispanic girl behind the desk reached for her phone. "Are you family?"

Catherine hesitated. "No, I'm not. Kayla asked her nurse to contact me. I came as quickly as I could."

"Let me talk to her nurse. It'll just be a minute."

Catherine struggled to catch her breath as she looked around the busy waiting room. The chairs were half filled with parents trying desperately to entertain their restless children. Two large metal doors beside the security desk slid open and a nurse walked through.

"Are you Catherine O'Grady?"

"I am."

"I'm glad you're here. Kayla's doing well. She's a delightful little girl. Let's go back and see her. She's really excited you were able to come."

Catherine followed the nurse through the green and yellow areas to the back of the orange area. The nurse held back a curtain as Catherine stepped around.

Kayla removed the ice bag from her forehead and bolted upright on the stretcher. Catherine engulfed her in her arms. They hugged and cried as the nurse closed the curtain around them.

Catherine brushed the hair from Kayla's damp eyes. "You've certainly grown even more beautiful over the past two years."

"I've missed you."

"I've missed you more than you know, precious. You remembered my cell-phone number."

"I've never forgotten it. I always kept the business card you gave me to put in my school bag. I've kept it in every school bag I've had. You told me to call you anytime. I thought this would be a good time."

"It's a perfect time." Catherine touched the large purple-blue bump over Kayla's right eye. "What happened, Kayla?"

"We were on our way back from the Wild Animal Park. One of the kids at the front said watch out for the raccoon. The next thing I knew we were skidding off the road and we all started screaming. I don't remember anything till a fireman put an oxygen mask over my face and kept asking me what my name was."

"How awful. You must have been so scared."

"I was. But the fireman and the paramedics were so nice. They kept telling me that I was okay and they were going to get me to the hospital."

Catherine lifted a loose strand of caramel-colored hair away from the bump. "That looks really sore. Does it hurt?"

"A little. My nurse told me to hold an ice bag over it to bring down the swelling." Kayla reached beside her and held a chubby brown teddy bear to her chest. "My doctor gave me this teddy bear. He said I've been so good."

The nurse appeared around the curtain and handed Catherine a box of tissues.

Catherine smiled, taking a tissue to dab her eyes. "Thank you. Kayla, have you heard from your mom yet? They said the school had been trying to reach her."

"She said she was going to be in family meetings all afternoon. You know she never answers her cell phone during those meetings."

Catherine turned to the nurse. "Alexis is a social worker at Mercy Hospital. Do you think we should call the hospital and have her overhead paged?"

"Absolutely. I'll take care of it."

The nurse disappeared around the curtain.

"Catherine, are you mad at me for having them call you?"

Catherine reached for the small hands gripping tightly to the teddy bear. "No, sweetheart. I can't tell you how much it means to me that you had them call me. I was scared to death when they said you were hurt. I'm thrilled to see that you're okay, besides that nasty bruise on your forehead."

"Do you think my mom'll be mad?"

"I think she'll be surprised to see us here together. What do you think?"

"She'll be really surprised, but I think she'll be glad to see you, too. I think she misses you. She talks about you sometimes. We lived with a woman named Barbara for a while but then she moved out. Mom's brought a few women home for dinner since then, but none of them have been like you."

Catherine didn't know what to think. For the past two years, she'd imagined Alexis living with Barbara. She couldn't understand why she felt so shaken to learn it was no longer true. "That's very sweet of you to say that. Why don't you lean back and I'll hold the ice over your bump. Do you have a headache?"

Kayla hugged the bear to her chest and leaned back in the stretcher. "No. My head just feels a little fuzzy."

Catherine placed the ice bag gently on Kayla's forehead.

"I thought you didn't love me anymore," Kayla said, "and that's why you moved out. Mom said her feelings for you changed and if anyone was to blame for what happened it was her. I was mad at her for a long time because I still love you and miss you."

Catherine touched the girl's bruised cheek. "Kayla, there isn't a day that goes by that I don't think about you. I loved you like a daughter. I still love you. Grown-ups have to do what's best for them in a relationship, but unfortunately the children of those broken relationships suffer as well. I'm sorry we both put you through that. I'm sorry this has been so difficult for you. Your mom and I couldn't see each other when our relationship ended and that meant I couldn't see you. It wasn't because I didn't love you, sweetheart. You've always had a very special place in my heart."

Kayla sat up in the stretcher and leaned into Catherine's arms. "I love you so much."

The nurse pulled the curtain back and Kayla and Catherine looked up.

"Olivia!" Catherine stood and stepped into Olivia's arms. "Thank you so much for coming."

She turned to the stretcher. "Kayla, I'd like you to meet Olivia. She's a doctor. She takes care of women, not children, but she wanted to make sure you were okay."

Kayla looked from Catherine's face to Olivia's then sunk deeper under the sheets and stared at her teddy bear. "Hi."

Olivia leaned closer. "Hello, Kayla. I'm sorry to hear about your bus accident. That's one nasty bruise on your forehead. Does it hurt really bad?"

"Not too bad."

"Well, I think you're really brave. If I had that bump on my head you'd sure hear me complaining and crying."

Kayla folded her arms across her teddy bear. "I'm not a crybaby."

Catherine stopped herself from telling Kayla to watch her manners. She wasn't the girl's mother; it wasn't her place.

Olivia raised her eyebrows slightly. "That's good to know. And it looks like you have a good friend there to make you feel better."

Kayla hugged her bear tighter and nodded reluctantly but didn't look up. Olivia glanced at Catherine.

Catherine squeezed Kayla's shoulder. "We'll be back in just a minute, sweetie."

The two women walked through the bustling emergency ward, out of Kayla's earshot.

Catherine took Olivia's arm. "I'm sorry."

"Don't apologize. That little girl hopes you'll come back into her life."

"I didn't fully understand how much I missed her until I saw her again. Especially with that terrible bump." She took a deep breath, distressed.

"What is it?" Olivia said gently. "There's something else."

Catherine had sworn she'd be honest with Olivia. That she'd never let communication break down between them. "Alexis and Barbara are no longer together. Kayla thinks her mom misses me."

Olivia was silent for a moment. "And how does that make you feel?"

"It makes me feel furious. Alexis broke my heart. She hurt Kayla, too." Catherine angrily brushed away a tear. She wished that fury were the only thing she felt.

"Is Alexis on her way to the hospital?"

Catherine nodded, searching Olivia's eyes. "I suppose I could leave before she gets here. But I may not see Kayla again for a long time..."

"Of course you should stay. Talk to Alexis. This is a perfect opportunity for you both to keep an eye on Kayla and talk about the things that have been troubling you for two years. Make sure Kayla knows you never intended to abandon her."

"Are you worried about me spending time with Alexis?"

Olivia took a breath. "I wouldn't be human if I wasn't worried, Catherine. You shared a commitment with her that you're not even sure you want with me. But I'd never stop you from doing something you need to do." She paused. "Did you finish the puzzle?"

Catherine fought back her confusion. It would be so easy to say that the pieces had arrived but she hadn't had time to fit them into place. "I did. It's a beautiful puzzle, Olivia. I just..."

Olivia nodded. Catherine could see the uncertainty in her eyes, beneath the strength. And she was responsible for putting it there, for denying Olivia a token of reassurance.

"Go back to Kayla, Catherine. You need to deal with your past before you can decide on your future."

Thirty

KAYLA SEEMED BOTH PLEASED AND ASHAMED when Catherine came back alone. They talked for a while, and then Kayla dozed off. Catherine watched her as she slept, filled with confusion and tenderness. She couldn't help imagining what it would be like to tuck this little girl into bed every night, as she had for three years. To watch her grow. She'd already missed two years of Kayla's growing up.

She stood up and paced, fighting back tears. Her heart belonged to Olivia. She felt that more strongly today than ever before. But her head was raging, telling her this was one of the reasons Olivia wasn't right for her. That Olivia didn't understand how much she longed to be a mother.

The curtain pulled back. "Oh, sweetie," Alexis cried, rushing to her daughter's side.

Catherine slowly backed away as Alexis hugged her daughter tight. Kayla's small arms went sleepily around her mother's neck. Alexis had let her dark hair grow longer, adding to her Mediterranean beauty. Catherine could feel the anxiety tighten her chest. Seeing mother and daughter together was so painful, flooding her with memories she'd once cherished. She tried to remind herself to stay calm and focused.

Alexis held her daughter's teary face in her hands. "Are you okay, baby?"

"I'm okay, Mom."

Alexis kissed her daughter's bruised cheek. "The principal told me what happened. I'm so grateful that you're all right. I was scared to death when I first heard."

"I was really scared when the bus started to swerve off the road. I don't remember a lot till the fireman started talking to me. He was really big and strong."

Alexis gathered her daughter into her arms. "I'm here now, baby. You don't have to be scared any more."

Kayla leaned back. "Catherine's here, too."

Alexis smiled. "I see that." She rose from the edge of the stretcher, stood before Catherine, and studied her face. "I know how difficult this must be for you, but thank you for being here for Kayla."

"I'm glad I could be. She's afraid you're going to be mad at her for calling me."

Alexis looked at her daughter. "I would never be mad at you for calling Catherine. You know that."

Kayla's sleepy eyes met Catherine's. "Are you going to stay for a while longer?"

"Yes, I am. I won't leave without saying good-bye, okay?"

Kayla nodded and drifted back to sleep, her teddy bar snuggled under her chin. Alexis settled again next to her daughter, and nodded toward the chair by the bed.

Catherine sat, feeling awkward. "I can't believe how much she's grown in the past two years."

"Neither can I. I want it to stop."

Catherine smiled slightly, looking at the woman who'd shared her life for three years. "How've you been?"

"Good, I guess." She caressed her daughter's cheek. "We've been talking about dropping by the bookstore to see you. I just haven't gotten the guts to do it."

Catherine didn't know what to say. The silence in the room grew heavier as Alexis stroked the hand of her sleeping daughter. "I know you don't think I really care, but how is Dana doing?"

"She's doing fabulous. She made it through her surgery and radiation with flying colors. She now divides her time between enjoying life, doing volunteer work with other breast-cancer patients, and the bookstore. She's really been an inspiration to other women."

"I can imagine. Dana was always such a strong woman." Alexis hesitated. "How've you been?"

"Good. The bookstore's booming and keeping me really busy."

"I can imagine." Alexis studied Catherine. "You look great."

"Thanks. So do you."

"I've missed you."

Catherine's calmness abandoned her. All her longing for family came rushing back, all her hurt at Alexis' betrayal.

"How am I supposed to respond to that? You broke my heart, Alexis. I may have been more involved with my mother's illness than was comfortable for you, but I still loved and needed you, and you betrayed that love."

"I'm sorry about what happened, Catherine. Please believe me. You were always one of the best things that happened to both of us. Kayla's the only one who fully appreciated you and your love." She paused. "Barbara and I are no longer together, if it makes a difference."

Catherine fought back tears. "Why would it make a difference? I've hated being alone, these past two years, but I haven't been able to trust enough to begin again. We had something I treasured, a partnership, a family, and you took it away."

"You're too wonderful a woman to be alone, Catherine. I hope you realize that soon, and open your heart."

"If I'm going to open my heart, I need to know the woman I love will be there for me. Through everything."

A flicker of exasperation crossed Alexis' features. Catherine remembered that exasperation, and the anxiety it always caused her. "I can't keep apologizing, Catherine. Life is complicated. Relationships are complicated. There's no such thing as forever. All we can do is give it the best shot we've got." Alexis shook her head, clearly regretting her outburst. "I'm sorry. My nerves are a mess. You can't imagine what a rough twenty minutes it was, between hearing that Kayla was hurt and reaching the hospital."

Catherine thought, *Yes I can.*

"It was awful to hear my baby was hurt. And it was a shock to see you here with her. But my heart leapt when I set eyes on you. It felt so right for you to be here."

Catherine looked at the little girl sleeping next to them. She saw something clearly, in that moment. She saw that Alexis might be capable of loving her again, sharing a home and life with her. Sharing the life of this precious child. But Catherine would always be wondering if another Barbara was waiting quietly on the sidelines of Alexis' life. Not because she was unable to forgive, but because Alexis was not the woman she needed, and never had been.

Alexis' beautiful, stormy eyes bore in on Catherine's. "I need to ask you this now, or I'll never forgive myself. Can you imagine us getting back together, and being a family?"

Catherine spoke without a moment's thought. "No, I can't." Alexis look startled. For the first time, Catherine knew in her heart that what she was about to say was true. "Because there's someone else. And she's right for me. Forever."

The color rose in Alexis' cheeks. Before she could speak, the curtain pulled aside and a kind-looking doctor stepped into the room.

Catherine and Alexis stood. "I'm Dr. Berman." He shook both their hands. "Which of you is Kayla's mother?"

"I am," Alexis said, looking worried.

Dr. Berman put his hand on her shoulder. "I think Kayla's going to be just fine, but we'd like to do a CAT scan of her head. Just to be sure there's no evidence of a skull fracture, bruising of her brain, or bleeding. And we'd like to keep her overnight, for observation. Does that sound all right?"

"Of course."

"You can come along, if you'd like."

Alexis looked at Catherine, her face a tangle of emotions. "Are you leaving now?"

"I'll be in the waiting room."

"Thank you."

Kayla was still sleeping as they rolled her away. Catherine felt as if she was losing her for a second time.

Thirty-One

ZOË OPENED THE FRIDGE DOOR and grabbed the Ziploc bag full of celery sticks. She set them on the counter then stretched on her tiptoes and reached into the cupboard for the jar of chunky peanut butter and a glass. As she stood before the water cooler and filled her glass, she noticed Olivia sitting alone on the patio.

Zoë gathered her snack and slid the sliding glass door open. Olivia rose from her chair and took the peanut butter and celery from Zoë's hands. "What're you doing up? It's almost ten-thirty."

Zoë sat in a cushioned chair beside Olivia. She gently rubbed her swollen tummy. "Nobody's taught your niece to tell time yet. She's hungry, therefore I must feed her."

Olivia held up the food. "She's asking for peanut butter and celery?"

"I hope so, because that's what I'm craving."

Olivia laughed as she twisted the cap off the peanut butter and handed it to Zoë. She opened the bag of celery and placed it on the small tiled table between them. "Is Echo sleeping?"

"Like a rock. She's exhausted. It's nice to see her sleeping so soundly, because in six weeks this little one will be keeping us both awake, I'm sure."

"I can't wait for the arrival of my niece."

Zoë grabbed a stick of celery and dug it into the peanut butter. She brought it to her mouth and crunched with glee. "Me, too."

"That's really gross, Zoë. It's amazing what a woman's hormones will do to her appetite."

"It's actually quite yummy. I can't wait to see what you'll be snacking on when your time comes to give me a niece or nephew. We'll see how gross this is to you then."

Olivia looked away and stared at the fire dancing in the flagstone fire pit.

"Have you heard from Catherine?" Zoë asked.

"Not yet."

"Are you worried?"

Olivia leaned forward in her chair. "I'm trying not to be. I'm glad she could be there for Kayla. She really loves that little girl."

"Are you worried about her spending time with Alexis?"

Olivia tugged aimlessly at the tie string at the waist of her black polka-dotted pajama bottoms. "How could I not be? What if she finds herself wanting that period of her life back?"

"Do you really think she'd want that? From what you've told me, Alexis broke her heart."

"They were together during the difficult, stressful time of Dana's diagnosis and treatment. Catherine might be wondering how different things could have been, under different circumstances. And she clearly misses Kayla desperately."

Zoë drank deeply from her glass of water and set it down on the table between them. "So it's a good thing she's connected again with Kayla. That doesn't mean she'll connect with Alexis."

"We'll see. I just hope I've let her know how much she means to me."

"You've let her know, Olivia. But you need to let her accept or reject your love in her own time." Zoë reached for the lid and screwed it back on the peanut butter. "For now, you need to stop wallowing in your own pointless fears. This is stressful enough for Catherine. The last thing she would want to hear is that you're sitting on our patio in your pajamas fretting about whether she's going to run into the arms of her ex-girlfriend. The reality of the situation is that Catherine is spending time with a little girl she loves who was just in a serious bus accident. In my mind that makes her wonderful, not a woman whose motives should be questioned."

Olivia looked at Zoë and smiled. "I think your surging hormones have made you a very wise girl."

Zoë gathered the peanut butter and bag of celery sticks. "Well, this wise girl has got to pee desperately so I'm going to say good night. Just promise me you won't sit here and drown in your self-pity."

"I think I've had enough wallowing for one night."

Zoë inched out of her chair. "That's what I wanted to hear."

Catherine paced the waiting room, feeling exhaustion and elation, hope and fear. She wanted to call Olivia, but she needed to know how Kayla was, first. She wanted to rush into Olivia's arms, declare her love. But Olivia had told her to deal with her past, and she knew she wasn't quite done with it.

Her cell phone chimed.

"Catherine, it's Alexis. Kayla's done with her CAT scan and they've moved her to the fifth floor.

"How was the CAT scan?"

"Perfectly normal. She has the healthy brain of a ten-year-old girl."

Relief flooded through her. "I'm so glad."

"Do you want to say good night to her? We're in room 504."

"I'll be right up."

As the elevator carried her higher and higher, a new hope began to grow in Catherine. She thought of the softness on Olivia's face when she talked about her soon-to-be niece. She thought of Sean and Amanda, the warmth of them snuggled against her when she read to them. She saw how one image of her future—the image of herself as a mother—had been keeping her from another one, a future filled with joy. Her life already was rich with children. And maybe Kayla, a child with a special place in her heart, could be part of that life, too.

Catherine stepped into room 504. It was a small private room; a mural filled one wall with big fluffy white clouds and rugged mountains surrounding a clear calm lake. Dora the Explorer sat at the lake's edge on a red-checkered blanket, enjoying a picnic with her best friend Boots.

Catherine sat on the edge of Kayla's bed and folded down the starched white sheet. "What a great room, sweetheart. And I'm so glad your head's okay. What was it like, to be in the CAT scan machine?"

"It was weird. It made funny clicking noises. But I knew Mom was there."

"That's always a good thing to know."

Kayla yawned and gripped Catherine's hand. "Are you going to stay awhile longer?"

"Just a little while. I won't leave without saying good-bye, okay?"

"Okay. Please tell Olivia I'm sorry for being mean to her."

"Maybe I'll let you do that. That's the least you can do, don't you think?"

"I guess."

Catherine watched her struggle to keep her eyes open. "Go to sleep and stop worrying. Everything's going to be all right. Trust me."

Kayla nodded her head and drifted off to sleep.

Catherine took a breath and turned to Alexis. "Alexis, I want to spend time with Kayla. Do you think that would be possible?"

Alexis looked taken aback.

"I meant what I said, about there being someone else. But I don't want to lose Kayla a second time."

Alexis was clearly struggling with her emotions. "Is that her name, this 'someone else'? Olivia?"

"Yes. Olivia." The name felt sweet on her lips.

"Kayla has missed you so much. She adores you."

"And I adore her. I want her in my life. But if you allow that, I don't want any animosity between us. I don't want to put her through that again. You and I would have to be decent to each other, especially when Kayla's around. Most importantly, I'm done with our past. I want to pour my energy into a future with Olivia."

Alexis extended her hand. "You have a deal."

Catherine took her hand. "Does this mean I can see Kayla?"

"You were always so good to her, Catherine. She would be elated to have time with you. These two years away from you have been really hard on her. It would mean a lot to me if you would be willing to spend time with her."

Catherine looked away as her eyes filled with tears.

"How do you think Olivia will feel about you spending time with Kayla?"

"I'll have to talk to her about it." Catherine fought back a flicker of worry. "But she has an enormous heart. I have to believe if it's important to me, it'll be important to her."

Alexis rubbed her hand along the arm of the wooden chair. "I always knew you would find someone, but it still feels like a kick in the gut hearing about Olivia."

"Good. I hope it felt like a kick in the ass, too."

Alexis laughed. "It's so good to see you haven't changed. I want you to be happy, Catherine. I hope Olivia's the woman you finally deserve."

Catherine reached for the tissue in her pocket. "I've certainly fought it hard enough, but I truly believe she's the woman I've been looking for my whole life."

Thirty-Two

THE NURSE CAME IN AT ELEVEN O'CLOCK for her hourly checks of Kayla. Kayla seemed grumpy at being disturbed in her sleep but happy to see that Catherine was still in the room. When the nurse left, Catherine moved to the side of the bed and kissed the little girl on the top of her head.

"Are you going home?" Kayla asked.

"Yes, I am. But the wonderful news is that your mom said we could see each other again."

Kayla's eyes got big. She turned to her mother. "Can we go to the bookstore and have hot cocoa with Catherine, Mom?"

"We sure can, sweetheart."

Kayla beamed. "I'm so glad that raccoon ran across the road in front of our bus."

Catherine laughed. "I'll call you at home tomorrow to see how you're feeling."

"Okay."

"Our big St. Patrick's Day celebration is on Saturday. Maybe if you feel better by then you and your mom can join us."

"That would be great."

Catherine leaned down and kissed her softly. "I love you. I'm so happy you're okay. Be a good girl and I'll talk to you tomorrow."

"I love you too, Catherine."

Catherine pulled the covers up tight to the little girl's chin, then slid off the bed and stood beside Alexis.

Alexis handed her a card. "That's my business card with our home number and my cell-phone number."

Catherine slipped the card into the pocked of her slacks. "Thank you," she said, blowing Kayla a kiss as she headed for the door.

Catherine pulled out of the hospital parking lot and hit the preset button on her cell phone for Olivia. A surge of excitement and anxiety swirled in her chest. She took a deep breath and told herself to stay calm. She made sure the earpiece was securely in place as she listened to the ring tone.

"Hello there."

Catherine swallowed hard. "Hi. Did I wake you?"

"Not in the least. I've been waiting for your call. How's Kayla?"

"She's doing great. They did a CAT scan, and everything looks fine, but they're keeping her overnight, just to be sure."

"I'm so glad she's okay. You must be physically and emotionally exhausted, Catherine."

"I haven't been this exhausted in a long time. But my mind is racing, too. There's so much I want to tell you, Olivia. May I come over?"

"You know the answer to that question. There's nothing that would make me happier. Where are you right now?"

"Fifteen minutes from your house."

"I'll open the garage door for you."

Catherine pulled her Volkswagen bug into the open garage beside Olivia's Escalade. Olivia was standing in the open doorway dressed in black polka-dotted pajama bottoms and a form-fitting black tank top. Catherine felt both thrilled and overwhelmed. There was so much she wanted to say, and she didn't know where to start. Everything had changed, and she wasn't sure she would be able to say why.

Olivia walked around the front of her vehicle and opened the driver's door. Catherine stepped out and caught her in a tight embrace. She slid her hands up Catherine's slender back and into her short chestnut hair. She breathed deeply as she inhaled her orange-blossom scent. "I'm so glad you're here."

Catherine looked into those tired amber eyes. "I'm so happy to be here with you." She leaned closer and kissed Olivia with slow, tender warmth.

Her head felt light as they pulled apart. "I've been trying to decide the whole time driving here what to say. You are everything I need and want. I love you, Olivia."

Competing emotions played across Olivia's beautiful features—joy, caution, relief, fatigue. "There's nothing I want to hear more than that." She smiled. "But maybe not in the garage. Let's go inside."

They walked through the quiet house. Olivia closed her bedroom door behind them and sat on the bench at the foot of the bed. "How was your time with Alexis?"

Catherine brushed her fingers across the elegant mahogany footboard, intensely aware of the thick duvet and inviting pillows on the bed. "I let go of that part of my past tonight,

Olivia. Everything changed. My feelings about family and relationship. My feelings about you."

Catherine stood before the blazing fire nestled in the white marble fireplace. The full moon winked back at her through the narrow windows flanking each side of the fireplace. She turned as she saw Olivia's reflection in the window, feeling an anxious fluttering in her stomach. "Spending this evening with Alexis made me realize what a favor she did for us by ending our relationship. It was never meant to last. What I want to last is what I have with you. I don't want to lose you, Olivia. I want a life with you."

Olivia stood and took Catherine's hands in her own. "I've wanted a life with you since the first day I saw you. I love you, Catherine. I want to spend the rest of my life sharing every day and every night with you."

"I'm here now, Olivia."

Olivia leaned her forehead against Catherine's. "This is certainly not how I imagined our first night together. It's been a tough evening, for both of us. I spent some uncomfortable hours, worried that I would lose you to Alexis."

Catherine touched Olivia's face. "Did you really think I'd go back to her?"

"The thought did terrify my mind this evening."

Catherine took Olivia's hands and held them close to her heart. "I'm sorry my actions tonight frightened you. I need you to believe me when I say you'll never lose me to Alexis or any other woman."

"I've been longing to hear that with every fiber of my being. But you're exhausted, Catherine. I don't want our first night to be clouded by your emotional time with Alexis and Kayla." Olivia brushed her lips against Catherine's, softly, slowly. "I drew you a hot bubble bath so you can soak and unwind."

"That sounds wonderful." They walked into the bathroom. Catherine stood before the gray-marble Jacuzzi, filled to capacity with foaming bubbles. Large candles flickered around the room, filling the air with the pleasing aroma of vanilla. Two thick lush white towels perched on the edge of the tub beside a big inflatable pillow. On one corner sat a clear tray with a tall glass of ice water, and a crystal bowl of plump strawberries and shiny green grapes.

Catherine turned. "What if I hadn't stayed?"

"I would have climbed in that tub myself, to ease my sorrow."

Olivia moved behind Catherine and slowly lowered the zipper at the back of her lavender dress, the material parting to expose flawless olive skin. She placed the open palm of her hand against Catherine's lower back and skimmed her hand upward. She brushed her lips against her slender neck and heard Catherine's rapt moan of pleasure. "I'm going to leave you to your bath, my darling Irish girl."

Catherine turned, confused. "You're leaving? You're not joining me?"

"I can't tell you how much I'd love to. But I think it will quiet your mind, to soak alone. It's been a long night for you, Catherine."

Olivia touched her fingertips to the loose neckline of Catherine's embroidered dress, then leaned forward and brushed her lips against her ear. "You should find everything you need in here."

Catherine gripped Olivia's waist tightly and pressed herself against her. "What I need is you."

"You're testing my self-control, Ms. O'Grady."

"Exactly my intention." Catherine grazed her lips along Olivia's jaw then took a step back, slowly slipping her arms from the sleeves of her dress and letting it slide down her body, revealing a lacy black bra and matching panties. She stepped out of the dress and carelessly draped it across Olivia's arm.

Catherine reached for the ties at Olivia's waist and slowly loosened the bow. She skimmed her thumbs along the smooth skin of Olivia's slender belly. Olivia took a shuddering breath and quickly pulled her close, crushing her lips to Catherine's with voracious need.

They pulled apart. Olivia leaned her face against Catherine's and struggled to catch her breath. "So much for self-control. But now I *am* going to leave you to your bath."

Catherine brought her hand to her mouth and touched her swollen, tingling lips. She watched Olivia move away, resisting the desire to reach out and pull her back.

Olivia turned as she reached the door. "I put a night-shirt on the vanity for you. My mom bought it for me from Victoria's Secret for Christmas, years ago. I'm more of a box-ers-and-tank-top girl. Goes to show you what my mother knows." She grinned and left.

Exhaustion washed through Catherine as the door clicked softly shut. She turned toward the tub. She couldn't remember when she'd last taken a truly luxurious bath. As she sunk into the bubbles, she realized that maybe Olivia did know what she needed, at least for right now.

Catherine placed the empty bowl of fruit on the saffron-yellow-speckled vanity and turned off the lights in the bathroom.

She stepped into Olivia's bedroom, surprised to see that it was empty, the inviting duvet undisturbed.

"Olivia?" she called out softly.

She heard Olivia's voice from down the hall. "In here."

Catherine made her way to her favorite of Olivia's spare rooms, the one with east-facing windows. Olivia was just finishing plumping the pillows on the queen-size bed.

"We're sleeping in here?"

Olivia looked up. "I'm getting the bed ready for you. Aren't you a beautiful sight in that nightshirt. Maybe my mother does know what I like, after all."

Catherine moved forward and grazed her fingers across Olivia's tanned chest. Olivia pulled her close. She rubbed her nose along Catherine's cheek. "You smell so fresh and clean."

Catherine slid her fingers along the waistband of Olivia's pajama bottoms, just beneath the soft cottony material. She touched her lips to Olivia's, slowly and sensuously. She heard Olivia's groan of frustration and kissed more deeply.

Olivia pulled Catherine closer with one hand, and slipped the other hand beneath the hem of the pink nightshirt, sliding it higher until it nestled on Catherine's naked hip.

She knew she could quickly lose herself in this kiss. She let her hand slide back down Catherine's thigh. "My darling girl, it's taking every ounce of my self-control not to tear this nightshirt from your beautiful body and make love to you." She took a breath. "If you still feel tomorrow that you want to spend your life with me, nothing will stop me. But tonight, just one more night, I think we should sleep in separate rooms."

Catherine searched Olivia's eyes, feeling both disappointed and grateful, aroused and exhausted. "Are you sure?"

Olivia nodded. "We're physically and emotionally drained. I need to know you've thought this through with a clear head. I believe in us with all my heart. But I need to be certain that you believe it, too."

Catherine slept more soundly than she ever could have imagined, with Olivia so close by. She woke at dawn, and padded softly down the hall to look in on the woman she loved. Catherine's chest swelled with warmth at the sight of Olivia sleeping so peacefully on her side, with the duvet barely up to her waist, the form-fitting black tank top accentuating her shapely arms and firm breasts. This was a sight she wanted to see every morning of her life. But Olivia had been right. Last night had not been the right time for their first night together.

Tonight, she felt certain, would be the right time, though she wasn't sure where the right place would be, to seal their future. She recognized that the differences between Olivia and herself couldn't simply be washed away by the wave of her love. Their pasts couldn't be washed away. Olivia might never feel comfortable joining her in a chapel, and there might be evenings when Catherine simply couldn't bear another story about cancer. But she firmly believed that those challenges, if faced with honesty, wouldn't undermine their partnership. They would only make it stronger.

She watched Olivia sleeping for several long minutes as a plan formed in her mind. Finally she returned to the guest room and snuggled back under the covers.

Thirty-Three

ZOË RUBBED HER ROUNDED TUMMY as Echo moved around the kitchen. The smell of brewing coffee was heavenly, but for now she would have to be satisfied with only the aroma. "Your daughter is tumbling around in here looking for some breakfast. My peanut butter and celery last night didn't sustain us."

Echo squished her face in disgust. "No wonder you woke up with heartburn this morning."

"I guess that means you don't want to hear what I'm craving for breakfast."

Echo sighed and draped an arm around Zoë's shoulder. "Let's hear it."

"A barbecued bratwurst smothered in sauerkraut and grilled onions."

Echo groaned. "That should give you and my daughter days' worth of heartburn. How about you start with some Raisin Bran and a bowl of strawberries and bananas?"

Zoë pouted effectively. "It's not the same, but at this point anything will do."

Echo brought Zoë's hand to her lips and kissed her knuckles. "I'll barbecue you a brat for dinner. Is that a reasonable compromise?"

Zoë's smile was infectious. "Your daughter and I'll love you forever for that."

"My daughter is going to come out screaming for a jumbo bottle of Tums."

They looked up as Olivia walked into the kitchen, buttoning the cuff on her pink blouse. Echo and Zoë spontaneously burst into applause.

Zoë stood and gave Olivia a sideways hug, the best she could manage with Chloe doing her somersaults. "I heard two sets of footsteps climbing our stairs not long after I left you last night. Sounds like Catherine chose the right girlfriend's arms to walk into."

"I'm thrilled by her choice. But don't break out the applause yet. She slept in the guest room last night."

Zoë looked distressed. "Did something go wrong? I felt so sure that she'd decided you were the one she wanted to be with."

Olivia smiled. "She did. It was just what I've been longing to hear. But she'd had such an emotional night with Kayla and Alexis, I wanted to be sure it wasn't just the emotion talking. I was the one who decided we should sleep apart."

Echo poured milk into Zoë's cereal bowl. "Are you regretting that decision this morning?"

"Of course. And not at all. Catherine and I have a lifetime ahead of us, if she truly feels today the way she said she felt last night."

Zoë reached for the bowl of fresh strawberries. "I'm amazed by your self-control, Olivia."

"It wasn't easy, trust me."

"I'm sure it wasn't. But somehow I think you'll be rewarded for your kindness. Is Catherine coming down to join us for breakfast?"

"She's sound asleep. But I'm hoping she'll be joining us for lots of breakfasts in the future."

Zoë turned to Olivia with shining eyes. "Catherine's one lucky girl. We're so happy for you."

"Nothing's for sure, Zoë. But I feel more hopeful than I have in a long time."

Thirty-Four

O LIVIA WALKED PAST THE PACKED PATIO of Cocoa Cream, feeling less at ease than she had this morning. She touched her jacket pocket, feeling the box inside. *Nothing's for sure.* Had she made the wrong decision last night, pushing Catherine gently away? Would it have made more sense to sweep her into her arms, as she'd wanted to do so desperately?

Catherine had sent her a text message in the middle of the day, asking her to come by the bookstore when she was finished working. Olivia had sent a message back, not wanting to be the one to initiate a real-time conversation. Was Catherine having second thoughts?

Olivia wove her way through the crowded tables of the café and headed through the bookstore, glancing cautiously down the aisles in search of Catherine. She met Dana emerging from of the Fiction and Literature sections.

Dana set the stack of paperback books down on the nearest table and stepped into Olivia's arms. "Well, hello there."

"Hello, Dana."

Dana held Olivia's hands. "You look lovely, as always."

Olivia felt tears sting unexpectedly at her eyes. She cherished the warmth that had grown between her and Dana in the past few weeks, and wondered what would happen if she and Catherine went their separate ways. She adored her dads, but her mother hadn't been a mom to her in decades, and Dana enriched her life in ways she'd never anticipated. She even felt the presence of Aidan and admired the true bond he and Dana had shared. She realized she'd fallen in love not just with a woman, but with a family.

"You're probably looking for Catherine."

"I am. I was instructed to make my way to Cocoa Cream."

"Why don't you go on back to her office. The door's unlocked."

Olivia squeezed Dana's hand and headed alone for the office. Catherine's orange-blossom scent lightly floated on the air, though no one was in the room. She left the door open and walked toward the small sitting area. She slipped into the nearest chair and stared down at the puzzle on the old chest. Lying on the center of the puzzle were two roses—one red, one white—on top of the velvet pouch Olivia had given Catherine with the first pieces of the puzzle. A card with Olivia's name scrolled across it in calligraphy lay beneath the roses and velvet pouch.

Olivia picked up the red rose and smelled its subtle fragrance. She picked up the card and noticed that the final piece, the Celtic knot, was still missing from the puzzle. Her heart lurched slightly. She slipped her finger beneath the flap of the card and tore it open. Inside was a card with a picture of two women walking along a beach arm in arm. Relief and happiness washed through her as she unfolded the letter inside.

My sweet Olivia,

Our beautiful puzzle is nearly complete. I left the final piece for you to add, so we could complete it together. I love the mystic fairies floating toward each other. The one hold-

*ing the Celtic four-pointed-knot pendant is you. I'm the one
reaching to receive it.*

*You were right: I needed to deal with my past before I
could embrace my future. You wanted to be sure that I still
feel today what I felt last night—that I want to spend my
life with you. And I do, with all my heart.*

*The Celtic knot symbolizes so much to me. It symbol-
izes eternity—the eternity I want to share with you. It
symbolizes eternal beauty, and the beauty I see in you.
You're strong-spirited with a beautiful soul. You, my darling girl, are full of integrity, faithful, loving, honest, and
trustworthy. I'm filled with excitement at the thought of
our future together. I'm drawn to you emotionally, intellec-
tually, physically, and spiritually. I look at you, I listen
to you, I see your smile, your eyes, your impish playfulness,
and I know I'm where I belong, next to you.*

*Seventeen days ago, you gave me a single pink rose,
and told me it signified friendship. Today I'm giving you
two roses, one red and one white, signifying both the passion and the purity of our love. They also symbolize our
distinct personalities, and the beauty we can create together.*

*At times in these past few weeks you've pushed me
beyond my comfort zone. Today, I want to push you a little
beyond yours, as a way for both of us to leave our pasts
behind and move into our future.*

*Our puzzle is complete. Now it's time for me to show
you how completely I love you. Two weeks ago you handed
me the velvet pouch to guide us on this journey. It will now
guide you to me.*

*Love always,
Your Catherine*

Olivia reached for the velvet pouch and loosened the strings, then slipped her fingers inside and pulled out the final piece of the puzzle. Carefully, tenderly, she snapped it into place and smiled. Opening the pouch wider, she pulled out a business card for the Hotel del Coronado. She turned it over and read, *A message awaits you at the front desk. I love you.*

Remembering her experience at the Coronado two years ago, a touch of confusion intruded into Olivia's happiness.

"I've never seen Catherine so full of nervous excitement as she was today."

Olivia looked up to see Dana standing in the doorway. "You knew she was planning something?"

"I've been sworn to secrecy."

Olivia smiled. She slid the business card into her pocket and grabbed the roses and card. "I better run, so I can learn for myself how the plan falls into place."

Thirty-Five

O LIVIA HANDED HER KEYS to the valet and headed across the balconied walkways. A wedding party hurried past as the bride struggled to keep from tripping on her train. Olivia wished she could still enjoy the Coronado the way she had before the unhappy weekend when Jessica had left her. Before then, she'd loved the Victorian grandeur of this historic landmark, the breathtaking ocean views, the opulence of the elegant lobby.

A young Hispanic woman smiled as she approached the reception desk. "Welcome to the Hotel del Coronado. How may I help you?"

"I'm Olivia Carrington. I was told a message would be waiting for me at the front desk."

The woman smiled as she reached into a drawer beneath her computer. "Yes, Dr. Carrington. Ms. O'Grady asked that we give you this key card. You're in one of our beautiful Signature Suites located in the Victorian Building. Your room is 201. Just head for those elevators behind you. Please don't hesitate to call us if you need anything, and enjoy your stay."

"Thank you."

Olivia studied the key card as the elevator rose to the second floor. Was Catherine turning the tables, giving Olivia a room of her own the way she herself had done for Catherine last night? Or was Catherine's plan for the two of them to spend their first night together here at the Coronado?

She located the door and slid in her key card. She stepped into the gorgeous living area of the suite, surrounded by plush couches. "Catherine?"

Hearing no response, she walked into the huge master bedroom, surprised to see her own suitcase sitting open on the king-size four-poster bed. The suitcase was empty except for a gift-wrapped package the size of a shoebox and a note written on a single sheet of pink rose paper. She picked up the note and read:

My sweet Olivia,

> *The last time you received a note in your suitcase it was an end. This is our beginning. This time, this place, this memory is for us to create. It's just about you and me exploring each other for the first time, with our pasts behind us. I'm ready to be your partner and your lover. I'm ready to be yours completely.*

Olivia looked up to find Catherine standing in the French doors leading to the balcony, dressed so elegantly in a floor-length sleeveless black dress. Olivia dropped the note into the suitcase as Catherine rushed into her arms.

Olivia brushed her lips against Catherine's flushed cheek, then stepped back and looked her up and down. "I'm so happy to see you. And yet I'm a little confused." She smiled mischievously and swept her arm to take in the beautiful room. "The Catherine O'Grady I know is not very comfortable with this kind of extravagance."

Catherine took Olivia's hands in her own. "That Catherine has turned into someone new. This one understands that on certain momentous occasions—not every day, mind you—extravagance is absolutely called for."

She grew more serious. "I hope this wasn't a mistake, Olivia. To remind you of a painful past. My desire was to put it behind us."

Olivia touched her lips to Catherine's forehead. "That's exactly what you've done."

"Celebrities, dignitaries, and American presidents have all slept in this beautiful hotel. I bet it has never housed a woman as extraordinary as you, Dr. Carrington."

"And you, Catherine O'Grady, take my breath away."

"I love you so much, Olivia. I want our first night together to be truly special. I want it to be a night we'll never forget."

"I'll never forget any moment I spend with you. I'll never forget walking into your office and reading that beautiful letter, especially since I was nervous you might be having second thoughts. Your interpretation of the Celtic knot moved me. I was touched that you allowed me the pleasure of placing the last piece in the puzzle."

"I wanted you to be a part of that journey."

"Since the day I met you we've been on an incredible journey. A journey I can only pray will last for all time."

"I truly believe the Celtic knot reflects our unity and timeless love and devotion to one another. I'd love to know what that puzzle means to you."

"I've always loved mythical fairies. When I first saw that puzzle I loved the peaceful imagery of those two beautiful creatures. I knew that the pendant the one fairy was handing the other was Irish but I didn't know what it meant or symbolized. I kept that puzzle in my office for a year, not knowing what to do with it. When a beautiful Irish woman came into my life, I knew I had to take a chance. I had to reach for my fairy princess and offer to share an eternity with her."

Catherine wiped at her tears. "You were brave to do that. Especially the way we first started off."

Olivia kissed Catherine's damp cheek. "Despite our beginning, you allowed us to talk and become friends. You graciously have allowed me these past two weeks to get to know you, and I've fallen so in love with the woman I met that fateful day. You, Catherine O'Grady, are the epitome of grace, self-respect, independence, and feminine strength. You have infinite ability to love and be loved." Olivia slid the soft pads of her thumbs beneath Catherine's moist eyes. "You're more beautiful than any fairy princess I've ever envisioned reaching for, and your gorgeous blue eyes convey every emotion you feel."

She reached in her pocket, pulled out a small velvet box, and placed it in Catherine's outstretched hand. "This is for you, my fairy princess."

Catherine held the velvet box in one hand and slowly opened the creaky lid. She blinked back tears and looked up at Olivia in shock. "It's stunning."

Olivia took the gold Celtic knot ring and slipped it onto Catherine's finger. "I want an eternity with you, Catherine."

"I would be honored to share an eternity with you."

Olivia held Catherine's face in her hands and kissed her softly, slowly, gently.

Catherine rested her forehead against Olivia's cheek. "Your beautiful ring will never leave my finger. I brought you a gift as well."

"I saw it. How did you find my suitcase?"

"I looked in your closet. I took the liberty of packing you a few things. I had a lot of fun going through your clothes."

Olivia laughed. "I'm sure you did. By any chance did you pack me a pair of boxers?"

"Tiny black boxers and my Christmas nightshirt. However, you won't need them for what I've planned for you."

"I'm really liking this plan."

Catherine handed the gift to Olivia. "A gift from me to you."

"I hate to unwrap it."

"There will be plenty more where that came from."

Olivia found the edges of the wrapping paper and carefully pulled off the tape. She slipped her finger under the paper and pulled back the edges, revealing an antique rosewood chest. "It's beautiful. As beautiful as the one on your desk."

Catherine touched Olivia's hands. "It's our wish chest. I want us to write down all our dreams and wishes and place them in this chest so they'll come true. My wish of finding my soul mate came true the day you walked into my life. I just needed some time to realize it was true. Go ahead and open it. I placed our first wish in there to get us started."

Olivia placed the chest in Catherine's outstretched hands. She carefully opened the antique lid and took the single piece of folded floral paper. She unfolded the small note and read. *I wish to bring my girl the highest joy and happiness from this day forth.* Olivia refolded the note and placed it back in the treasure chest. She grabbed the hotel pad of paper and slipped her pen out of the inside pocket of her jacket. She wrote quickly on the pad and tore the top sheet off. She held it up for Catherine to read.

I want forever with you, my Irish girl. Catherine smiled as Olivia folded the note and placed it in the chest. Catherine slowly closed the lid and placed the chest on the Victorian table beside her ring box. "Forever starts right now."

Olivia gathered Catherine in her arms and stared into her deep blue eyes. "You're my greatest joy, Catherine O'Grady. Being here with you makes me so incredibly happy."

She touched her lips to Catherine's with soft, caressing kisses. She felt Catherine's tongue seeking hers and eagerly surrendered to her search.

Olivia opened her hands wide and slid them across Catherine's lower back. She found the opening of her dress and traced her fingers along the subtle recess of her spine. Catherine trembled in her arms. "Just before you make me completely lose my mind, I should probably call the girls and tell them I won't be home tonight."

Catherine smiled. "I called them today and asked for their permission and their blessing to be with you."

"Wow. What was their response?"

"They were ecstatic. Zoë said I had their permission to ravage you senselessly."

Olivia shook her head and laughed.

"I also called Brady and Austin. They were moved that I asked for their blessing. They welcomed me to the family."

"That was really sweet that you called everyone."

"I know how much it means to me to have my mother's blessing. She loves you so much, Olivia, though I made her swear not to let on what I had planned for tonight. I wanted to make sure everyone we both loved felt the same way. I would've called your mother, but somehow I don't think that would have been as important to you."

Olivia grinned. "That's for sure. But I'll call her and tell her I've grown very fond of the Christmas gift she sent me." They both laughed.

"Dana insisted on calling Ruth, too. You officially have tomorrow morning off work."

"A miracle! You Irish women think of everything."

Olivia stood back and skimmed her fingertips up Catherine's arms, feeling her shudder beneath her touch. "I was just wondering if you'd hoped to wear this incredibly sexy dress anywhere outside this room tonight, because I've got this deep need to see it draped across a chair and have you draped across me." Olivia brushed her lips along the slender column of Catherine's neck.

Catherine arched her neck and basked in Olivia's sensuous kisses. "I put it on for you. That gives you the right to do whatever you want with it."

Olivia scraped her nails lightly down Catherine's back and luxuriated in her breathless gasp. "Will I be ruining your dinner plans if you find it pooled at your feet in a few seconds?"

Catherine caught her breath. "I ordered us chicken salads and lemon meringue pie for dinner. Champagne is chilling on ice. Room service was kind enough to put the food in our fridge. They set a table on the balcony for us whenever we're ready to eat." She grazed her lips against Olivia's upturned jaw. "Are you hungry?"

Olivia swallowed hard. "Food is the last thing on my mind right now."

Catherine stared into those glistening amber eyes. "Let's see if I can't empty your mind." She leaned closer and took Olivia's lips with uninhibited lust. Olivia's tongue demanded entrance and Catherine was happy to oblige.

Catherine stepped back from the kiss. This was a moment she'd been waiting for her whole life. "My heart belongs to you," she whispered.

She slid her hands along the lapels of Olivia's mocha jacket and slipped it from her shoulders, letting it drop to the floor. She traced her fingertips around the top silver button on Olivia's silky black blouse before slowly releasing each one. Soon the blouse was on the floor as well. Catherine placed her hands on Olivia's abdomen and circled her belly button with her thumbs. Olivia's quick indrawn breath incited Catherine's zealous yearning as she slid her hands up her tummy and over the edges of her bra.

Olivia closed her eyes and breathed deeply. "Darling, you're sadly mistaken if you think I can stand here and take this much longer. I thought I'd warned you that patience is not one of my strong suits."

Catherine skimmed her hands across the smooth, tanned skin of Olivia's chest. She slid her palms over her ribs and luxuriated in her tenacious arousal. "I'm here to teach you patience, my love."

Catherine hooked her fingers beneath the lacy material and released the center snap. She slowly eased the bra away, staring at Olivia in wonder, then leaned forward and trailed moist kisses between Olivia's breasts. "God, I want you." She slid her hands up the tense muscles of Olivia's back and touched the tip of her tongue to her taut nipple. Olivia struggling to stay standing.

Catherine unhooked Olivia's belt and eased her slacks to the floor. "I've never seen a woman as incredibly gorgeous as you." She hooked her fingers beneath the lacy material of Olivia's panties and slid them over her hips, then knelt as Olivia stepped out of them. She looked up into Olivia's sizzling amber eyes as she ran her hands over her firm thighs, touching her slightly parted lips to her warm belly. Olivia groaned with impatience, took Catherine by the shoulders, and guided her to her feet.

"My turn," she said, crushing her lips to Catherine's with brazen insistence. She moved swiftly behind her and covered her tilted neck with suckling kisses, then gripped the zipper of her dress and slid it down, aroused to see that Catherine was wearing no bra. In moments, Catherine's dress and panties had joined Olivia's clothes on the floor.

The two women stared at each other, awed, each catching her breath. "Baby, I can't stand this much longer," Catherine said.

A voracious hunger filled Olivia as she walked Catherine back to the bed and laid her down on the cool pastel yellow sheets. Olivia eased herself over Catherine and slipped between her parted thighs. "I want you so much."

Olivia touched her lips to the sensitive spot behind Catherine's ear then slid lower and tantalized her peaked nipple. Catherine bowed against her eager mouth, weaving her fingers into Olivia's hair. Olivia moved to her other breast and brushed the hardened nipple with long even strokes of her tongue, emboldened by the moans of Catherine's staggering need. She allowed the nipple to slip from her mouth and moved to lean above Catherine. She looked into the stormy, half-opened eyes and kissed her softly. "I love you."

Catherine threaded her fingers behind Olivia's neck and held her head in her hands. "I love you, my darling."

Olivia supported herself on one arm as she cupped Catherine's breast in her hand. She stroked it in a light circular motion and heard Catherine inhale sharply. She slid her hand over her ribs as Catherine writhed beneath her.

"That feels wonderful," Catherine murmured.

Olivia slid her hand across her hip and over her belly as Catherine spread her thighs wider. "You feel so incredible, my love."

Catherine groaned. "Please touch me."

Olivia grinned widely. "That would be my pleasure, my impatient little lover" Olivia skimmed her fingertips along the inside of Catherine's thigh as Catherine strained toward her in open invitation. She combed her fingers through Catherine's thick, dark mound and slipped through her silky wetness.

Catherine cried, "Oh, my God, darling, yes."

Olivia touched the tip of her tongue to Catherine's up-turned jaw and down her neck. "You feel so amazingly wet, my love." Olivia explored her velvety folds before plunging her fingers deep.

Catherine gasped Olivia's name as she rocked her hips against her hand, falling into an abyss of raw bliss.

Olivia slipped from deep within her and found her rigid center, stroking with light, smooth strokes.

Catherine felt a hypersensitive coil of tingling tension build at the point of Olivia's touch and spread throughout her tense muscles. She bunched the bed sheet in her fist as she felt herself slipping from the precarious ledge of this blistering ecstasy. The tightly coiled tension sprang free as she screamed Olivia's name.

Olivia slipped back inside Catherine's pulsing center, basking in her release. She brushed soft kisses across her lover's flushed, hot cheek.

Catherine leaned her face against Olivia's and sighed heavily. "Oh, my God, that was amazing."

"It certainly was."

Catherine smiled as she traced Olivia's lower lip with her thumb before touching the tip of her tongue to Olivia's. Catherine indulged in Olivia's wetness against her thigh as she eased Olivia onto her back and slid over her.

Their hands naturally entwined as Catherine brought Olivia's arms above her head and stared into her shimmering eyes. She pressed herself firmly between Olivia's thighs. Their tongues chased and clashed.

Catherine kissed Olivia's shoulder, then the bend of her extended arm. Olivia sighed with pleasure as Catherine kissed her way to their joined hands. "Darling, you're going to shatter my sanity, aren't you?"

Catherine took Olivia's fingertip into her mouth and sucked on it deeply. She leaned back over Olivia's face. "Not shatter it. Just shake its foundation."

Catherine held Olivia's hands just above her head and ground her hips tight to Olivia's. She loved Olivia's lusty cries of delight as she kissed her curved neck and down across her chest. She moved to her firm breast and traced the outline of her nipple. She brought their entwined hands down to Olivia's sides and laid a trail of kisses between her breasts and down her belly.

Olivia squirmed beneath her as each stroke fueled a slowly brimming keg of raw ecstasy. She spread her thighs wider as she felt Catherine slip lower between her legs and touch her lips to the inside of her thigh. She turned her face into the pillow. "Oh, God, babe, that feels amazing."

Catherine's tongue found her essence and Olivia cried out in pleasure. She gyrated her hips to Catherine's rousing caresses as the mounting tension flowed and built. She felt her heart pounding in her chest as she battled to prolong this agonizing ecstasy.

Catherine lightly scraped her teeth across Olivia's erect center as her lover groaned wildly and thrust one final time against her. She felt Olivia's thighs tense against her shoulders as a surge of wetness bathed her tongue.

Olivia held her breath and tensed her legs as she felt the geyser tense and explode, ripping her from the grip of sanity. She heard a scream that vaguely sounded like her own voice as she soared free on wings of pure bliss.

Catherine slowly moved upward into Olivia's outstretched arms. She buried her face in the softness of Olivia's neck and felt her arms completely encircle her. She watched Olivia's chest heave with each breath and finally settle to a peaceful rhythm. She wished to keep this moment between them forever.

"That was incredible," Olivia said finally.

Catherine raised her head and touched her lips to Olivia's. "I've dreamed of this moment with you. But I never dreamed it could be this beautiful."

"Sweetheart, you and I are only beginning to create something beautiful," Olivia said as she tasted herself on her lover's lips for the first time.

Catherine eased herself over Olivia and kissed her with slow, gentle, caressing kisses. She straddled her thighs and traced her tongue down the smooth skin of her neck and into the recess of her collarbone

Olivia held her tight against her. She thrust upward against her parted thighs and indulged in the sight of them so intimately entwined.

Catherine leaned in closer and teasingly touched her lips to Olivia's. She basked in Olivia's frustrated groan as she outlined her upper lip with the tip of her tongue and eased away.

Olivia glared at her with half-open eyes. "If you're trying to toy with me, I hope you're prepared to deal with the consequences of your actions." The challenging look in Catherine's sky blue eyes was all Olivia needed. She eased herself up into a sitting position, then gripped Catherine's hips and pulled her in tight on her lap.

Catherine raised herself up on her knees and held Olivia's shoulders. "You turn me on, Dr. Carrington." Catherine eased her tongue between Olivia's swollen lips as she felt her lover's fingers skim across her bottom and dip into her wetness.

Catherine closed her eyes and thrust herself rhythmically onto Olivia's hand, driving her fingers higher and deeper. She felt the caress of Olivia's thumb as she fought to hold on to this moment before it shot her from the tenuous ledge of wondrous rapture.

Olivia watched in awe as Catherine threw her head back and basked in erotic bliss, then slowed her rhythm and thrust one final time. Undulating spasms gripped Olivia's fingers as Catherine cried out her astonishing release.

Olivia slipped her fingers out slowly and eased Catherine back onto the bed, securely in her arms.

"I think I've died and gone to heaven," Catherine said.

Olivia kissed the top of her head. "I'm right there with you, darling."

Catherine watched her long eyelashes rest peacefully against her smooth skin. "Have I emptied your mind enough to interest your tummy in a chicken salad?"

Olivia peeked through a half open eye. "Can we eat in bed?"

Catherine eased over her and gently nipped at her shoulder. "I thought we already did."

Catherine and Olivia sat on the balcony, entwined on a lounge chair, looking out across the twinkling grounds of the Coronado to the moonlit Pacific.

Olivia sighed. "I never would have thought both my heart and my belly could be so full at the same time."

"Mmmm."

Olivia glanced at her lover. "Are you okay, sweetheart?"

Catherine hesitated a moment then turned to meet Olivia's eyes. "I have something to ask you."

"Of course."

"I talked to Alexis about letting me spend some time with Kayla."

At the mention of Alexis' name, Olivia's heart lurched slightly.

"She agreed. But I wouldn't want to do it unless you felt okay about it."

Olivia battled a moment with her emotions. She hadn't wanted Alexis to intrude on this night. But this wasn't about Alexis, she told herself. It was about Kayla. It was about a little girl Catherine loved.

"Catherine, that's wonderful. I'm so happy for you. And once you feel Kayla's ready, I'd love it if the three of us could spend time together, too."

Catherine's face lit up. "Do you really mean that? Because that's all I've been able to envision, since Kayla came back into my life—the three of us together—but I wasn't sure you'd feel comfortable with it."

"Of course I do. She's important to you, Catherine. I'd love to get to know this little girl you love so much. Besides, it'll give me a chance to whip her for being so mean to me."

Catherine laughed. "Give her a chance to apologize before you decided if she needs a good whipping."

"If you insist."

Catherine leaned closer and touched her lips to Olivia's. "You're even more amazing than I thought."

Thirty-Six

CATHERINE LAID HER VELVET GREEN DRESS across the bed of the light-filled room that she was starting to think of as her own. She and Olivia had been together every night since the Coronado, alternating houses. Wednesday night they'd stayed at Olivia's, and Catherine had spent two happy hours reading in this room after Olivia left early for work, the light pouring in the east-facing windows. On Thursday they'd spent a wonderful, cozy night at Catherine's, leaving Catherine deeply happy. She'd also been happy to come back last night to Carriage House Lane, to sit around the fire with Echo and Zoë. She still didn't know how the issue of two homes would resolve, but she was too content to let it worry her.

Wearing only her lacy black bra and matching panties, she walked back across the hall and into the bathroom as Olivia finished blow-drying her hair.

Olivia turned and smiled, a look of longing in her eyes. "You'd better put on more than that, darling, if you expect me to get moving here."

Catherine moved closer and dipped her fingers just beneath the waistband of Olivia's bikini panties. "Do you think my mother would be upset if we didn't show up for the celebration today?"

Olivia gathered her close and floated her hands across her tight bottom. "I think your mother would disown us if we didn't show up, so you better get dressed and stop distracting me."

Catherine touched the tip of her tongue to Olivia's upper lip. "You're right. We probably should get going. We have enough time to stop by my place and drop off our bags on the way, if you like."

Olivia moved her hands up Catherine's smooth back and along her ribs. She brushed her lips along her cheek. "I vote for spending those extra fifteen minutes just holding you and tasting your delicious skin."

Catherine arched her neck and sighed with deep pleasure. "I second that vote."

The sultry, lilting harmonies of three Irish sisters filled the air as Olivia and Catherine walked into the bookstore. The coffee shop was filled to capacity as everyone crammed in to listen to the songs of a distant land.

Olivia leaned in close to Catherine's ear. "This is amazing."

"It truly is. The O'Hara sisters have such beautiful voices. They always draw a huge crowd."

Olivia skimmed the soft pad of her thumb across her smooth cheek. "Darling, you really know how to throw a party."

Catherine touched her wrist. "To be here with you and the people we love means so much to me."

Olivia touched her lips to Catherine's. "Happy St. Patrick's Day, my love."

Catherine's eyes filled with tears as she slipped into Olivia's embrace.

"Speaking of the people we love, Ruth and Dana are waving at us," Olivia said. She gripped Catherine's hand and they made their way across the room to the two beautiful middle-aged women.

Olivia tapped the button on Ruth's lapel and laughed. "This is perfect for you. 'I'm not Irish, but kiss me anyway.' Guaranteed you'll get a ton of mileage from that."

Dana placed a shiny beaded shamrock necklace around Olivia's neck. "I have one for you, too." She slipped her fingers beneath the lapel of Olivia's jacket and secured a green pin with white lettering that read, "Kiss me, my girlfriend's Irish."

Catherine beamed. "Perfect." She looked at the crowd around them. "Where's everybody?"

Dana leaned closer to be heard over the music. "Laura's running around trying to keep up with the customers. Kevin's entrenched in a beanbag in the children's section with Amanda and Sean. Zoë and Echo just left to go to the bathroom, and Brady and Austin are listening to the harpist. The last time I saw Maya she was perched atop the grandfather clock glaring at the crowd."

Dana heard a young voice shout her name. She turned as Kayla rushed into her arms.

Dana hugged the little girl tight. "Kayla! Oh sweetie, I've missed you so much."

Kayla kissed her cheek and leaned back. "I've missed you too, Dana."

"Look how much you've grown!"

Kayla smiled. "I'm almost as tall as my mom's shoulder." She grew more somber. "I'm so glad you're not sick anymore."

"Me, too, Kayla. I feel very blessed to be healthy again." Dana brushed the hair away from the dark purple bruise on

Kayla's forehead, noticing Alexis standing warily to the side. "I was so scared when I heard about your accident. How are you feeling?"

"I'm much better. My headache's gone, but I have to be careful when I brush my hair, 'cause I always manage to bump my bruise."

"That must hurt. I'm so glad you're here with us again."

"Me, too. I was so happy when Catherine came to see me in the hospital. Mama says things happen for a reason and I think my bus accident was supposed to bring us all together again."

"I wish it didn't have to happen that way, Kayla, but I do believe you were always meant to be a part of our lives."

Dana turned and put her hand on Olivia's shoulder. "Olivia, I believe you've met Kayla but not her mother. This is Alexis. Alexis, Olivia."

Alexis nodded and extended her hand. "I guessed as much. It's good to meet you."

Olivia hesitated a moment. "I'm glad to meet you, too. Kayla means so much to Catherine."

Kayla looked up at Olivia a little shyly. "I'm sorry I was mean at the hospital."

Olivia smiled broadly at the little girl. "And I completely forgive you. A hospital room is an awful place to meet some-one new."

Happiness washed through Catherine, seeing the two of them together. "Kayla, neither you or your mom have met Dr. Ruth Ratcliff. She's the doctor who took care of my mom's breast cancer and she's a very special friend of ours."

Alexis cautiously approached. "Hello, Dr. Ratcliff."

Ruth formally shook her hand. "Hello, Alexis." She turned to Kayla. "Hello, Kayla. I've heard so many wonderful things about you from Catherine and Dana. They both love you very much."

"I love them very much, too. Thank you for taking care of Dana. I was really worried about her."

"It was my pleasure to take care of Dana. She's very special to me as well, and I'm just as thrilled as you are that she's a breast-cancer survivor."

Olivia reached for Kayla's hand. "Come on, Kayla. Amanda and Sean are waiting for you in the children's section. They're excited about seeing you again. And Catherine bought these amazing beanbag chairs that just about swallow you up when you sit in them. Let's go check it out."

Kayla gripped Olivia's hand and looked up at her mother. "Is it okay if I go with Olivia, Mom?"

"Of course. I'll come join you in a minute."

As Olivia and Kayla walked away hand in hand, Catherine noticed Laura making her way through the customers. She joined the group and gave Alexis a look of sheer disgust. "You've got a lot of balls stepping back into our house, Alexis, after the way you hurt Catherine."

Catherine touched Laura's arm. "Please, Laura. Don't. Not here. Not now."

"I'm not going to make a big scene. You've had this out with her, but your mom and I've never had the chance. I know I promised to be civil so I'll just say this once and be done with it."

Laura turned to Alexis. "What you took from her has been given back to her tenfold. You'll never hurt her again because you'll never get close enough. I'll make sure of that. The only reason you're standing here today is because of your daughter. It certainly isn't because of any of us wanting you back in our lives. You've been given a second chance, Alexis.

Try not to screw it up this time. I'll be watching your every move. You'll never get away with being the hateful bitch you were two years ago. Do you understand me?"

Alexis stood ramrod stiff. "I understand."

"Good." Laura turned to Catherine. "I had to get that off my chest so please don't be angry with me. Now, I have a customer on the phone regarding a special order he placed with you. He says he needs to speak to you."

Catherine took her hand and turned to include the others. "Laura had every right to say what she needed to say. But now I want to ask all of you to give us the opportunity to have Kayla back in our lives without any more conflict. Let's bury the past and start again."

Laura grunted. "Fine. I don't want to make things difficult for you, so I'll behave. Just make sure she does the same."

Catherine smiled. "That's a deal. Lets go talk to our customer." Catherine turned to her mother. "While I'm gone, please be nice. I don't want any bloodshed in the bookstore. Alexis has been kind enough to bring Kayla to share in our celebration."

Dana glanced at Alexis. "It's my bookstore, too. I can splatter a little blood if I want to."

Catherine glared at her mother. "Ruth, I'm counting on you to keep the peace. I'll be right back."

They all watched Catherine and Laura walk away.

Alexis took a deep breath. "It was a mistake coming here."

Dana shook her head. "You didn't think for one minute that we would pretend that the pain you caused Catherine never happened."

Alexis faced Dana. "I guess I hoped we could all let go of the past, as Catherine requested."

"Well, you're wrong again, Alexis."

Alexis tightened her grip on her purse strap. "I talked this out with Catherine, Dana. I don't know what more I can say to you."

"There isn't anything you could possibly say to rectify what you did to my daughter. You never deserved her. Luckily, she somehow managed to survive everything we put her through, and is stronger and wiser."

"You're right, Dana. I never deserved Catherine. I truly loved her, but she chose to be there for you instead of me, and I couldn't deal with that."

"I understand that my breast cancer was difficult for all of us, but I never imagined that you would use it as an excuse for your own selfishness."

Ruth put her hand on Dana's arm. "I think this is the point where I step in to keep the peace."

Dana took a breath. "If it were my choice I'd never want to see your face again. But Catherine is a much better person than I am, and she's found a woman who loves her far more than you ever could have. She wants to rebuild a relationship with Kayla while she's building her life with Olivia. I respect and admire that. From this moment on, I'll be civil to you because I too adore your daughter. But I'm only going to tell you this once. Don't you ever hurt my daughter again. Have I made myself perfectly clear?"

"Crystal clear. Now, if you'll excuse me, I'm going to join my daughter."

Ruth shook her head as Alexis walked away. "Wow. I think that's the first time I've really seen your fiery Irish temper. You had me scared."

"Maternal instincts bring it out in me." Dana sighed. "Maybe I was too hard on her. I felt responsible for a very long time for what happened between her and Catherine. They were fine until my cancer."

"Don't even say that. You're in no way responsible for what Alexis did. And Catherine's right, it's time to put the past behind us. Your daughter's future looks wonderful right now. Yours does as well. And I never, never, would have wished breast cancer on someone as beautiful, generous, and honorable as you, but I'm deeply grateful you came into my life."

They looked into each other's eyes for several long moments before Ruth broke the spell. "Now, let's head to where the harpist is playing. Then I want to get a front row seat for those Irish dancers you hired."

Dana didn't like the grin on Ruth's face one bit. "Behave yourself, Dr. Ratcliff, or you might just see that tough side of me again."

Ruth took her hand and guided her forward. "Promises, promises."

Thirty-Seven

CATHERINE UNLOCKED HER FRONT DOOR and stepped aside. Olivia wheeled her suitcase into the foyer as Catherine turned the lights on and shed her jacket.

Olivia stepped down into the sunken living room. She dropped into the overstuffed beige suede couch and leaned her head back, sighing with pleasure. "I love your house, Catherine. Every time we come here I just want to snuggle into this couch with you forever."

Catherine slipped in beside her. "With our busy lives, I'm just grateful to steal whatever moments we can to snuggle." She laid her head on Olivia's shoulder. "Are you tired, baby?"

"Not tired, just overwhelmed. Please tell me right now if every St. Patrick's Day will be like this, because I don't know how many more I can survive."

Catherine slipped her hand into the opening at Olivia's blouse. "Did O'Sullivan's do you in?"

"Oh, my God. I've never been in such a high-spirited restaurant in my life."

"But then again you've never been to an Irish pub on St. Patrick's Day."

"This is very true. Can you believe I lived thirty-six years without anyone expecting me to drink green beer like it's water?"

"Wasn't it so much fun, darling?"

Olivia slipped her hand along Catherine's neck and deep into her hair. "It was more fun than I've had in a really long time and completely overwhelming, but that's just how my life has been since the moment you stepped into it. Over the past several years I've had so little time for pleasure. You bring that to my life with a vengeance. That's truly a gift you give me."

Catherine leaned closer and kissed her sweetly and gently. "I'm glad. I had such a wonderful time with you tonight. You made my St. Patrick's Day so special."

Olivia pulled an envelope from her pocket and handed it to Catherine. "Speaking of this incredible day, I've got something for you."

Catherine removed a shimmering green-and-yellow St. Patrick's Day card and smiled at the leprechaun on the front. Inside was a slip of paper inscribed in large bold script. "Paris trip voucher for Catherine O'Grady." She looked at Olivia. "What's this?"

"You told me that you wished for your mom's continued good health and Cocoa Cream to grow and prosper. Those dreams have been fulfilled. You also dreamed of seeing Paris. I want to fulfill that dream with you. I'm going to take you to Paris as soon as we can book the time off together. That's my tenth-anniversary gift to you."

Catherine blinked several times. "This is way too generous a gift, Olivia."

"I seem to remember you telling me that certain events deserve extravagance. This is one of those events. You've worked hard for the success of Cocoa Cream. I want to celebrate with you. I love you and I want to spend lazy days sitting by the Seine River with you breaking bread, crumbling cheese, and sipping on expensive French wines. I want to fill our days with museums and magnificent churches. I want to spend the nights making love to you in a high-ceilinged Parisian hotel room."

Catherine leaned her face against Olivia's, realizing she was finally ready to accept such generosity. "I love you so much. It would truly be a dream come true to go to Paris with you, darling."

"If it'll make you feel any better, I'll let you buy the baguettes."

Catherine laughed. "I might even spoil you with crêpes and marzipan."

"Now, let's not go crazy."

"This has truly been a magical day. Do you care to end it with a bath? I can't offer you the elegance of your Jacuzzi, but I think my simple bathtub will be quite cozy."

"Lead the way."

Catherine slipped into a tiger-print negligee and matching string bikini panties. She checked herself in the mirror before dimming the lights in the bedroom. She removed several thick pillows from the bed and turned down the duvet. She lit the sugar-cookie candle on her dresser and checked the room one more time.

She walked into the bathroom as Olivia finished washing her face. She marveled at her exquisite body. Her long shapely legs disappeared into black silk boxers that fit snuggly against her tight bottom. Her lines were sleek and fit beneath a black tank top that hugged firm peaked breasts. Catherine had to restrain herself from tearing her clothes away, especially when she saw the look of longing in Olivia's eyes. "Are you hungry, darling?"

Olivia smiled. "Not after Mr. O'Sullivan's delicious fish and chips. However, the sight of you in that gorgeous negligee certainly makes me very hungry for you."

Catherine moved closer. "I was hoping I might be able to stimulate your appetite."

"You do more than just stimulate me. You drive me absolutely wild." Olivia gripped the tiger-print negligee by the hem, eased it over Catherine's head, and threw it toward the bedroom. Catherine felt like liquid fire in her arms as she guided her backward and leaned her against the glass wall enclosing the shower. "You're so incredibly beautiful. I want you more than I've ever wanted anything in my life." She cupped each breast in her hands, leaned down, and grazed Catherine's nipple across her wet lips before sucking her in deeply.

Catherine felt the cool glass against her back as the heat of rapture flushed through her body. She didn't know how much longer she could remain standing as she held Olivia's head close.

Olivia moved to her other breast and bathed it with her tongue. Feeling Catherine's knees buckle, she wrapped one arm around her waist and molded the other hand to her firm, heaving breast. She brushed her fingertips down her flat belly and around her belly button before slipping inside her panties. She watched Catherine's tense expression as she threaded her fingers between her velvety folds. Catherine's guttural cry infused Olivia with urgency and she dove her fingers within her.

Olivia fed Catherine's torrid need, kissing her deeply for several long moments, then slid from within her and caressed her rigid essence. Catherine moaned heavily against her lips as each stroke fueled her desire.

Catherine thrust one final time against Olivia's exploring fingers before releasing a cry of pure erotic bliss.

She slowly opened her eyes. "Oh, my God, darling, that was incredible."

Olivia smiled. "I love making love to you."

Catherine grazed her lips across Olivia's. "I think I'll take you to O'Sullivan's on a regular basis."

Catherine grabbed the large inflated pillow from the bathtub and one of the large fluffy white towels. She laid the towel open on the vanity and leaned the pillow against the mirror.

Catherine guided Olivia back up against the gray marble vanity. She crushed her lips to Olivia's and chased her tongue with a ravenous obsession. Then, in quick succession, she pulled the tank top over Olivia's head, slid the boxers down to her feet, and slipped out of her own panties. She loved the unrestrained yearning in Olivia's bright eyes as she moved in tight between Olivia's parted thighs and pressed herself intimately against her.

Olivia thrust against her and cried with exquisite plea- sure as Catherine slid her hands along her sides and over her breasts. Her nipples strained against the palm of her hands as she caressed them.

Olivia lifted herself up to sit on the towel on the vanity and lay back against the inflatable pillow. Catherine moved with her and pressed herself firmly between her parted thighs. She loved the feeling of Olivia's legs wrapped around her waist as she gyrated against her wetness.

Catherine slid her hands along her thighs and onto her hips. She devoured her lips with an insatiable hunger and plundered her with her tongue in a desperate race for fulfill- ment. Catherine loved Olivia's cry of surrender as she slid her fingers through her wetness and deep inside her.

Olivia tightened herself around Catherine's fingers. She groaned with pleasure as Catherine slowly slid from within her and caressed her in her own wetness in small light circles.

Catherine felt Olivia tightening her thighs around her and tensing with each light stroke. She pressed her lips to her closed eyelids and across her cheek. Olivia quivered at her fingertip, then went very still before releasing a deep guttural cry of ecstasy, the tension rippling between her thighs then surging like seawater crashing over a breakwater.

Olivia held Catherine tight in her arms as she battled for each new breath. "Oh, my God, that was amazing."

Catherine buried her face in Olivia's warm neck. "You feel so wonderful."

"You're an amazing lover, Catherine O'Grady. If I knew that Irish women were like this I would have taken a trip to Ireland years ago."

Catherine laughed. "Think of how much money I've saved you in travel expenses." She kissed Olivia's cheek. "I think we might be ready for bed now."

Olivia kissed her way along her neck. "Who needs a bed when this countertop seems just perfect for our needs?"

Thirty-Eight

CATHERINE REMOVED THE LAST of the books from the packing box, collapsed the box, and stacked it with the others. Gathering the books in her arms, she turned to the wall unit, which was nearly filled now with familiar volumes and other treasures—lush plants she'd nurtured since they were small, photographs of her and her parents.

The room where she'd spent her first night at 25 Carriage House Lane was slowly being transformed into her study. After a month of living between two houses, she and Olivia had decided that the big house would be home. Olivia had been very sweet not to push her, and the decision now felt abundantly right, particularly as Catherine moved more and more of her own home to Carriage House Lane. The house that once seemed overwhelming now seemed just right for four people, with a little one arriving soon.

Catherine was amazed by how quickly she and Olivia were growing closer, growing into each other's lives. She actually found herself enjoying Olivia's somewhat more messy style, a sign of her energy and commitment to her life outside the home. And it helped that she would have her own orderly room to retreat to.

All week they'd used Olivia's Escalade to swap furniture back and forth between the houses. All the pieces Catherine truly cared about were now here. Several couches and chairs from the living room at Carriage House Lane, plus the bedroom furniture from the room that was now her study, fit perfectly at Catherine's house, which they planned to rent furnished to two intern friends of Olivia's. The puzzle was falling into place surprisingly easily now that they were committed to making it work.

She heard Olivia's key in the door, and then her musical voice. "Honey, I'm home."

Catherine hurried happily down the hall and met Olivia as she reached the top of the stairs. "And what a lovely sight you are, Dr. Carrington." Catherine brushed her hands along her jeans and slipped into Olivia's arms, feeling the tension in Olivia's muscles. She kissed her softly and looked into her eyes, alarmed by the exhaustion and sadness she saw there. "What's wrong, sweetheart?"

Olivia forced a smile. "Geez, I can't hide anything from you."

Catherine took her hand. "You're too sensitive to hide your feelings from me. Let's go in our kitchen. I'll pour you a glass of orange juice and you can tell me what's troubling you."

"That sounds great."

They walked hand in hand down the hall. Catherine had moved everything from her own small kitchen into the one in her and Olivia's suite. She doubted they'd prepare more than breakfast or snacks here, but it made her happy to be surrounded by her favorite dishes and utensils.

Olivia watched Catherine dig into the fridge and pour her a tall glass of orange juice. She slipped onto a familiar stool from Catherine's house and touched the leaf of a lush fern. "Are you making headway with your unpacking, babe?"

Catherine handed Olivia the glass. "I'm nearly finished with the books. Wait till you see how great the wall unit looks." Catherine touched Olivia's face. "Thank you for being so patient with me about this decision. I'm so excited by the way things are coming together."

"The rewards have been worth it." Olivia took Catherine's hand and pulled her close. She kissed her softly and deeply.

Catherine held Olivia's face in her hands. "What's wrong, darling? What happened this afternoon?"

Olivia set the glass on the counter and pushed it away. "Emma never showed up for her two-o'clock appointment this afternoon."

Catherine frowned. "What happened?"

"I had my receptionist call her house. One of her sons answered. He'd gone to pick her up and bring her to our appointment when he found her down on her kitchen floor."

Catherine brought her hand to her chest. "What does that mean?"

"Emma was dead when he found her. There was no evidence of foul play so they're speculating that she had a heart attack or stroke."

Catherine stared at Olivia in disbelief. "Why didn't you call me and tell me as soon as you heard?"

"I couldn't tell you at the time, Catherine. I had a waiting room full of patients I still had to see. I would've loved to pick up the phone and share this with you, but I couldn't."

Catherine stepped away from Olivia as tears filled her eyes.

"I'm sorry, babe," Olivia said. "I know you cared about Emma."

"She was such a darling. She had such strong will to fight her cancer."

"I know. I wanted to help her fight."

"If that first idiot doctor had helped her instead of blowing her off, this may never have happened."

"You don't know that. We still don't know the cause of her death. Echo did a very thorough study of Emma's cardiac function and she cleared her medically for surgery. If it was a stroke, it may have happened whether she'd had earlier surgery or not."

"Are you defending his actions?"

"I'd never defend another physician for not giving a woman a chance to fight her breast cancer. We'll never know how well she would have done had I done the surgery."

"Emma died not knowing, either," Catherine said, her voice harsh.

"This is my career, Catherine. I deal with life and death issues every day. But I don't want to see you upset like this. It's not healthy for you or us."

"I see. Because I'm not so skilled at dealing with cancer and death and dying like you and my mother then I'll be only allowed to share a selective part of your life. Well, that's not good enough, Olivia. I thought we'd committed to sharing our lives completely. I've got news for you. Us mere mortals feel what we feel. If something upsets me, I show it. When someone I care about dies suddenly, I'm deeply shaken. You're telling me she was found this afternoon and you're just telling me now and you're expecting me to handle this rationally."

Catherine walked to the window and stared out into the yard.

"This isn't the type of news we share on the phone, Catherine. I wanted to be with you when I told you."

Catherine turned back to Olivia. "You've had time to process your feelings, Olivia. I haven't. I need time to deal with my feelings, too. I'm sorry I've disappointed you with my anger. I'm sorry I can't be supportive to you right now when I'm in shock."

"This tears me up too, Catherine. I've been so afraid that you would feel like I failed you."

"The only way you failed me, Olivia, is by not letting me be me. You've underestimated my faith in you. I've seen you in enough professional situations to know you're an outstanding physician. You not only care for your patients physically, but emotionally and spiritually. I'm responding to the loss of a wonderful woman who I only met for an hour. She touched my life in that space of time. I need you to have more faith in my emotions. I need to be able to expunge my feelings and know that you won't worry that I'm attacking you personally or professionally."

She took a breath, then went on. "I told you in the beginning I don't know how you deal with this, day in and day out. You're a much stronger woman than I am. I'm going to ask you to let me lean on that strength once in a while, and to learn from it. I did my best to deal with losing my father. I learned so much about my mother and myself as we went through her breast-cancer treatments. Both of you are extraordinary women. I admire and envy both of you. You're the type of women who teach by example. I may not be ready to help cancer survivors myself, but I need to hear your stories and be allowed to react to them, as the emotional woman I am. You need to tell me now if that's more than you're prepared to deal with, because I want you completely, Olivia. Not just the safe, selective parts of your life."

Olivia reached for Catherine and pulled her in tight. "I love you so much. I love your fire. I never want you to stop sharing your feelings with me. I just want so fiercely to protect you."

"You can't protect me from life, Olivia. I want you to make me a part of your life. Good and bad. I want to be there for you but I need you to give me a chance to react to such horrible news and digest it. I promise I'll put it in the proper perspective and never let it affect us."

"You're way more woman than I ever dreamed of falling in love with, my mere mortal. I'm more than willing and eager to share my life with you. But I'm so sorry about Emma. I wanted to help her. For her and also for you."

"I know. And you did help her. You have no idea the strength your office gave Emma by just giving her that appointment. You gave her hope before she even met you. I just pray that she went quickly and painlessly."

"I hope so, too." Olivia watched the tears fall from Catherine's deep blue eyes. "I'm sorry about squelching your emotions. I promise not to let that happen again. I love everything about you and I never want to stifle the emotional woman you are."

Catherine brushed at her tears. "Good, because I plan on tormenting you with my emotions for as long as we both shall live."

Thirty-Nine

CATHERINE CAREFULLY PULLED OUT of the Cocoa Cream parking lot and merged with the evening traffic. She secured the earpiece in her ear and hit the preset button for Olivia's cell phone.

Olivia picked up on the second ring. "Hello, sweetheart. Are you coming to take me away from all this madness?"

"I'd be delighted to."

"I'm just finishing my rounds on the fifth floor. I should be done within the hour."

"Sounds great. I'll go talk to my dad. Why don't you call me when you're done?"

"That would be my pleasure. Don't forget to light a candle for my grass-skirt fantasy. I'm still waiting for that one to become a reality."

Catherine laughed. "Dr. Carrington, one of these days I'm going to shock you by coming to bed dressed only in a grass skirt with a tall icy Mai Tai in my hand."

"If that's how prayers work, sign me up."

"There's a little more to prayer than that, darling. Go take care of your patients, and I'll see you soon."

Catherine smiled as she disconnected the call. She liked it that Olivia felt comfortable speaking lightly about prayer.

She truly believed that their differences—including their feelings about faith—could make them stronger as a couple, more balanced. And she knew that Olivia was happy for her when she sought out the rituals that soothed her.

Catherine walked through the main entrance of the hospital and past the lineup at the coffee cart. Just past the gift shop, she saw a familiar figure standing at the end of the hall, seemingly lost in thought as she stared out the huge glass wall to the hospital courtyard. It was Natalie, the daughter of Olivia's patient. Catherine could still feel Natalie's pain the day they'd talked in the bookstore. She'd thought about the young woman and her mother often, and Olivia had kept her up to date on their progress. Natalie's mother had been admitted to the hospital a couple of days before, for something to do with her diabetes. Luckily it didn't sound too serious.

Catherine thought about saying hello but didn't know if she could bear any more sadness. It had been less than a week since Emma died, and she still felt shaken. She slipped into the chapel and felt embraced by feelings of stillness and solace. Dropping a twenty-dollar bill in the collection box, she reached for a stick, lit the end, and stared at the flickering flame. "I could pray for her, Dad, or pray with her. What would you like me to do?"

Catherine lit the nearest candle and felt a surge of strength and guidance. She smiled as she slipped the stick into the jar of sand. "I was afraid you were going to feel that way. Well, here goes." As she stepped out of the chapel, Natalie was still standing at the end of the hall.

The young woman glanced over as Catherine approached and broke into a smile. "Well, hello there."

"Hi, there. I noticed you here a few minutes ago, but you looked lost in thought and I wasn't sure I should disturb you."

"I was just watching the sparrows play in a puddle of water. How are you?"

"I'm great. More importantly, how are you and your mom doing?"

"Up and down." Natalie shrugged, but she seemed relaxed. "Mom started chemo as an outpatient last week, but she had a lot of problems with nausea and dehydration, and her blood sugar's been really low. Dr. Carrington decided to hospitalize her to get the vomiting and blood sugar under control, and to rehydrate her."

"Wow. That's a lot to handle. But you seem in better spirits than when we met."

"I'm in much better spirits, in spite of everything. I can't tell you what a difference it made to talk to you and your mom. Ever since then, Mom and I just talk about anything and everything that's on our minds about her illness. It's helped us both to understand we have the same fears. It's brought us a lot closer and helped us to be stronger these last few days. I feel I can be there for her and she feels comfortable talking to me instead of feeling she has to protect me."

"That's wonderful."

"It really is. Dr. Carrington's been great. She's been wonderful to my mom and never tires of answering our millions of questions. She makes you feel like you can conquer anything when she's on your team."

Catherine laughed. "Don't tell her we both see her as Joan of Arc. We'd hate for it to go to her head."

"I won't if you won't. Hey, would you like to meet my mom? The nurses were helping her back to bed. She's been up in her chair most of the day. I just came down here to get out of their way."

Catherine hesitated only a moment. "I'd love to."

Olivia stood at the bank of elevators on the fifth floor and flipped open her cell phone. Sensing a familiar presence, she glanced up and saw Catherine walking down the hall, a delightful smile on her glowing face.

Olivia tilted her head. "I'm sorry for staring, but I'm a little confused. You're certainly as beautiful as my girlfriend, and you walk like my girlfriend, but my girlfriend is the last person in the world I would expect to see strolling down this hall."

The doors slid open to an empty elevator and Catherine stepped inside, taking Olivia's hand and pulling her along. "I'm trying my best to show you that I'm not totally hopeless." Catherine hit the button for the main floor. The doors slid closed as she leaned into Olivia and kissed her softly. "Hi, beautiful. I was just talking to Natalie and her mom. And before you think I acted on my own, my father made me do it."

Olivia stumbled back against the wall of the elevator and raised her arms to the sky. "I love you, Aidan. You've given me one incredible girl. It doesn't look like I'll have to trade her in for a newer model after all."

Catherine narrowed her eyes at Olivia as the elevator doors opened. "You can barely keep up with this model, Dr. Carrington. You'd be wise to learn to enjoy this ride, if you know what's good for you."

Olivia leisurely looked Catherine up and down as they walked toward Olivia's office. "I've already bought tickets for unlimited access to your ride, sweetheart. Nonrefundable, nonexchangeable. I'm in for the long haul."

"Glad to hear it. I'll let you know how many tickets you need to redeem for tonight's ride. In the meantime, my mom and Ruth are waiting for us at Luigi's Pasta Emporium and they're starving."

Olivia unlocked her office door. "You can tell me on the drive all about this close encounter of the third kind that led you to my patient and her daughter."

Catherine smacked Olivia's shoulder. "Stop making fun."

"Are you kidding? I'm so proud of you I can barely stand it."

Catherine followed Olivia into her office and closed the door behind them. She leaned back against the closed door and grabbed Olivia by the lapels of her crisp white lab coat. "Why don't you just take a moment to show me how proud you are of me."

Olivia crushed her lips to Catherine with raw yearning. Catherine's raspy moans fueled Olivia's passion as she pressed her hips between Catherine's parted thighs. She trailed her moist lips along Catherine's slender neck and suckled at the base of her throat. "How hungry did you say Ruth and Dana are?"

Catherine arched her neck against the door. "Damn."

Olivia slid her hands along Catherine's thighs and beneath her purple suede skirt. She gripped her hips and pulled her tight against her. "Whose bright idea was it to invite them to dinner, anyway?"

Catherine thrust against Olivia. "I'll never make that mistake again."

Olivia leaned her face against Catherine's and laughed. "I'm going to tell your mother you said that."

"Not if you know what's good for you." Catherine brushed her lips along Olivia's full lower lip and kissed her softly. "Let's skip dessert, okay?"

"Deal. Just remember where we left off." Olivia's cell phone chimed at her waist. She flipped it open. "It's Echo. Hóla, chiquita."

"Hey, Olivia. I hope you guys are ready because your niece looks like she's ready to make her grand appearance."

"What? Where are you guys? What's happening?"

"Zoë had her first contraction about thirty minutes ago and it was a whopper. She needed to pee once it settled down and when I got her to the bathroom her water broke. We're on our way to the hospital now."

"We'll meet you there, Echo. Please drive carefully."

"I will. See you soon, Olivia."

"You sure will." Olivia ended her call. "Zoë's in labor."

Forty

OLIVIA STOOD LOOKING OUT at the dawn sky. After little Chloe had been placed at Zoë's breast—with Catherine and Echo watching in exhausted awe—Olivia had touched Catherine's hand, whispered, "I'll be right back," and slipped out of the room. For some reason she didn't want anyone seeing the emotion she was feeling, not even Catherine.

It had been a long night and a difficult labor. She remembered feeling this same fatigue when she'd been an intern, except then her patients had been battling disease or recovering from crippling injuries. She felt no heavy-heartedness this morning, only exhausted joy. Zoë had wanted to be a mother ever since she was a little girl. Olivia was only now recognizing how truly powerful and irrepressible that longing was. At the end of this long night, Zoë's pain was gone and a miracle had come into the world.

Olivia's mind went back to the hours they'd spent in the cheerful birthing room. She and Echo and Catherine had been at Zoë's side the entire time, breathing with her, joking with her between contractions, massaging her neck, bringing ice to quench her thirst. In that room, Olivia had felt the power of family in a new way, and especially the bond between Echo and Zoë. This child would complete and deepen their love.

Toward the end it had become a blur, Zoë yelling out unabashedly as Echo and the doctor urged her to push, and finally the boisterous wail as the baby made her entrance in the world.

"It's all right, little Chloe," Echo had said when the nurse placed her wailing daughter in her arms. "You're here now. We've been waiting our entire lives for you. I know that was a bit of a rough ride, but imagine how your mom must feel."

The sky outside was growing lighter, promising to be a beautiful spring day. Olivia took a deep breath and rubbed her own neck. She needed to let all this settle in her heart and mind, but something was changing inside her as this new day dawned. Her understanding of Catherine was deepening, her love deepening. She felt so grateful that Catherine had faced her issues and doubts, allowing them to be together. She knew she needed to address fears of her own—ones she'd barely acknowledged—if she was going to embrace their love to the fullest. Already she felt those fears melting away.

She walked back down the hall and into the joy-filled room. Catherine looked up, her beautiful face questioning where Olivia had been, but also fully absorbed in the scene in front of her. Zoë was propped up in bed, her daughter cradled on her knees as she took in every detail for the first time. She touched her daughter's face, each tiny finger, her smooth chest.

"You're so beautiful." She kissed Chloe's head then looked up beaming at the three women surrounding the bed. "Our baby's finally here."

Olivia secured Chloe in her baby carrier. Catherine covered her in a thick pink receiving blanket and tucked it along her sides. "There you go, precious. You're ready for your ride home. Your honorary grandmas Ruth and Dana are on their way up with your stroller. Your grandpas Brady and Austin are parked at the main entrance to take us all home so we can show you your beautiful nursery."

Olivia slipped her finger into Chloe's tiny fist. "Prepare yourself, kid. This is what it'll be like all the time. I hope you knew what you were doing when you chose those two as your parents, and this family as your family."

Echo stared at her daughter in awe. "I still can't believe she's here."

Zoë skimmed her hand across Chloe's thick crop of dark brown hair. "She certainly made her appearance known to the world."

Echo kissed Zoë's temple. "Like mother, like daughter. Before we leave, there's something I want to give you." She pulled a long slim package from her purse and handed it to Zoë.

"What's this, sweetheart?"

"Just something I've been waiting nine months to give you."

Zoë tore the wrapping paper off the package. She lifted the lid and a smile lit her face.

Echo took the necklace from the box and linked it behind Zoë's neck. The gold pendant depicted two parents and a child linked in a circle of love. "This is a symbol of all of us in this room. I had the jeweler place each of our birthstones in the link that joins the parents and child. It's the love in this room that made this child possible, and that same love will raise her." Echo held Zoë's face in her hands. "I feel so blessed to have you and there is no greater gift you could ever give me than our daughter."

Catherine felt the tears stinging her eyes. So many blessings had come into her life in the past two months, so many changes. Her beloved Olivia, first and foremost, and the wonderful family she brought with her. Her mother's five years as a survivor; Cocoa Cream's ten years of success. Kayla was back in her life bringing so much energy and enthusiasm, and she felt closer to Laura and her family than ever. Her life was unfolding, not entirely in the ways she envisioned, but with more fullness than she ever had dreamed.

Olivia slid her arm around Catherine's waist, leaned in close, and spoke softly so only Catherine could hear. "One of these days it'll be *our* little one we'll be bringing home, into this big family."

Catherine turned to Olivia, her beautiful eyes surprised and bright. "Are you sure?"

"As sure as I've ever been of anything in my life. As sure as I am of you."

Breinigsville, PA USA
15 November 2010
249373BV00001B/73/P